A BOOK BY
TRIPTI DUTTA

AF107287

From Another PERSPECTIVE

BlueRose ONE
Stories Matter
NewDelhi • London

BLUEROSE PUBLISHERS
India | U.K.

Copyright © Tripti Dutta 2025

All rights reserved by author. No part of this publication may be reproduced, stored in a retrieval system or transmitted in any form or by any means, electronic, mechanical, photocopying, recording or otherwise, without the prior permission of the author. Although every precaution has been taken to verify the accuracy of the information contained herein, the publisher assume no responsibility for any errors or omissions. No liability is assumed for damages that may result from the use of information contained within.

BlueRose Publishers takes no responsibility for any damages, losses, or liabilities that may arise from the use or misuse of the information, products, or services provided in this publication.

For permissions requests or inquiries regarding this publication, please contact:

BLUEROSE PUBLISHERS
www.BlueRoseONE.com
info@bluerosepublishers.com
+91 8882 898 898
+4407342408967

ISBN: 978-93-6783-413-8

Cover design: Daksh
Typesetting: Tanya Raj Upadhyay

First Edition: January 2025

To my Grandparents

Bakshi Bisheshawar Nath Dutta

&

Bakshi Sheela Dutta

We miss you!

As my dream unfolds into reality, I extend my heartfelt gratitude towards my publishing partner, Bluerose Publication, and the entire team. Kevin, you Really held the ground for us; Sakshi, thank you for weaving all the threads to bring this vision to life. Sherya and Dhruvi, your kindness and patience throughout this journey have been truly invaluable, and Tanya and Daksh, the book radiates sheer beauty.

PRELUDE

"Bibi! Raza Sahab is worried and hasn't eaten a bite since morning," Aslam, a devoted servant of the household, expressed with concern etched upon his wrinkled face. His cracked voice, white hair, and hunched back spoke of years gone by as the master's home had cradled him since childhood. Clad in grey pants and a blue shirt, he had woven himself into the fabric of this family.

Rida cast her gaze upon the patients lingering outside and exhaled softly. "Aslam Kaka, kindly brew some tea for us. I shall join Raza Sahab in just a few moments." She bestowed a warm smile upon him before turning her attention back to the waiting patients.

He nodded and shuffled towards the kitchen, where he brewed the tea with a careful hand, adding just the right amount of sugar until it reached the perfect hue and aroma. Arriving with the household elders after the India-Pakistan partition, he had devoted his life to serving the family.

As he handed Rida the tray of snacks and tea, he advised, "Baba should avoid TV for a while." His eyes, filled with worry, met hers.

She smiled in reassurance, "Ji, kaka, I will try to switch off the TV."

"Raza Sahab! Iqbal has the virus, so call him individually and tell him not to come to the factory for another week. Also, ask Manager Sahab to take leave as his daughter is getting married next week," Rida instructed anxiously, placing the tray before her husband.

"Raza Sahab, what troubles you? You haven't even gone for a walk; I fear your diabetes may spike." She observed her husband, whose gaze remained glued to the news channel covering the Indo-Pakistan war.

"Raza Sahab!" she called, raising her voice.

He turned to her as she nudged him, offering a cup of tea.

"You cannot simply sit here and worry about Asad," she added, her own concern mirroring his.

"How is Amina?" he asked, shifting his attention to Rida.

"She is fine; the pain may start any moment," she replied with a reassuring nod.

"Alhamdulillah! Alhamdulillah! Tell her Asad will return as soon as the war ends," he said, a calm smile gracing his lips.

"Yes, we must have faith in Allah, Raza Sahab!" she affirmed warmly.

"I believe Asad will be back to cherish his perfectly healthy child. He has long awaited this blessing." Raza sipped his tea, his gaze still fixed on the TV.

"I remember when they were children. How can I forget meeting Amina for the first time? She came to Islamabad with her father to compete in a race— that was the day someone dared to break Asad's record. Asad was astonished to see a girl run so swiftly, and he spoke of it all week."

"Yet, Asad was even more surprised when Muhammed Zia-ul-Haq proposed Amina's hand in marriage. General Sahab believed they would make an extraordinary pair, training together for the Olympics one day. Amina's parents were delighted to have an army officer as their son-in-law." He chuckled at the memory.

Suddenly, the phone rang, jolting Raza and Rida from their reverie. Raza hesitated before answering, his hands trembling as he lifted the receiver.

"Asalaamwalakum!" the voice on the other end greeted him.

"Walikum Aslam!" Raza Sahab replied, his heart racing.

As the conversation faded into growing silence, Raza's complexion drained of color, fear overtaking him. Rida, sensing his distress, rushed to hold his hand.

"Aslam Kaka!" she shouted.

Servants hurried inside, assisting Raza Sahab to a sofa.

"Bibi, Amina Bibi is in pain," a maidservant exclaimed, rushing in with urgency.

"We cannot tell her anything right now," Rida answered, anticipating her husband's silent question.

"She deserves to know, Rida," he replied, his eyes brimming with pain.

"Yes, but not when she is bringing a new soul into this world. As a doctor, I implore you to keep it from her until she delivers and recovers," Rida insisted, steadied by resolve. She stood, instructing Shaheen, the maid, to gather essentials before heading to Amina's room. Amina's relief was palpable upon seeing Bibi Rida.

"Everything will be fine, Amina; just breathe deeply," Rida encouraged, taking Amina's hand.

Amina followed the guidance, managing a smile through the agony, knowing her husband would soon return with uncontainable joy upon seeing their child.

"Amina, just a few more pushes, and the baby will be here," Rida soothed, her words a balm amid the chaos.

Amina's cries echoed through the house, a stark contrast to the looming shadow of grief that enveloped them.

"It's a boy, Amina! A beautiful baby boy," Rida announced with joy.

Amina smiled faintly, touching the newborn, still connected by the umbilical cord.

"He is so beautiful, just like his mother," Rida beamed, lifting the child for Amina to see.

Exhausted, Amina closed her eyes. "Baji, did he call?" she whispered.

Tears welled in Rida's throat, threatening to spill, yet she replied with composure, "Yes, he called. He will be back soon!"

But Amina, whispering something inaudible, drifted into unconsciousness.

Rida broke into tears, overwhelmed at the bedside.

"Bibi!" she was interrupted by the midwife, who had cleaned the baby and wrapped him in a soft cloth.

"Mashallah! He is a bright light for us," she said, kissing his forehead and cradling him.

"Bibi! Take the child downstairs to Raza Sahab; I'll tend to Amina," the midwife instructed, and Rida nodded.

In the drawing room, Raza held the child, kissing him amid sobs. "He is my son; I will raise him as my own."

"Did you tell Amina?" he asked, his eyes red.

"No, she is unconscious; I could not bear to tell her the truth," Rida whispered, tears escaping her.

A servant entered, announcing, "Amina Bibi is awake."

Rida turned to her husband. "It's better if you tell her. I have already lied; I cannot face her now."

He rose, cradling the child tightly, and entered the room. Amina, noticing her brother-in-law, instinctively covered herself with her dupatta.

"It's alright, Amina. You are like my daughter. Don't trouble yourself," he said gently, offering her the child. The baby smiled in her lap, while he took a seat beside her.

"Amina, I must tell you something," Raza began gravely.

"Ji, Bhai Jaan," she looked up, her apprehension growing. "What is it?"

"Amina, the child in your arms needs you to be healthy, and what I must say pains me deeply," he continued.

"Bhai Jaan, please say he is coming home," she urged, dread pooling in her heart.

"Bache, he has departed to another world, leaving us behind," Raza revealed, his heart breaking.

Amina gasped, clutching the baby tightly as sobs wracked her body. Rida, seated beside her, placed a comforting hand on her head.

"This baby needs you to be strong; you are our family, Amina. Asad believed in your strength, and that's what made him fierce at the border," Rida reassured her, patting her back.

"Baji, I was strong because he was my strength. Now that he is gone, I don't think I can breathe," Amina cried.

"For this child, you must find strength; Asad would want you to be strong," Raza implored gently.

"He has no right to expect anything from me, Bhai Jaan. He is not here to father his child or love him. How can I fulfill his role?" Amina sobbed, burying her face in Rida's chest.

Feeling helpless, Raza exited the room.

Rida tried to console Amina, but the baby began to cry, sensing his mother's grief; Amina's sobs lessened, exhaustion weighing her down.

"Raza! Raza, come here!" Rida called, panic rising.

Raza rushed back in; horror etched across his face. "Amina! Amina, get up, beta."

But Amina lay still, lifeless.

"No, Amina bache! This is unfair to your child!" Raza cried, despair consuming him.

Together they sat beside her, engulfed in shock, helpless against the tide of loss.

CHAPTER 1

I sat upon the balcony, a silent observer of the rain as it wove its spell upon the city and the bustling thoroughfare of Ajmer Sharif Dargah. Years have slipped by, like whispers in the wind, yet the scene remains unchanged—the familiar rented room, the same balcony where we once gathered, gazing toward the Dargah, seeking inspiration and fortitude. But today, I found myself alone, the rain cascading beneath a blush-hued sky, filling me with an exhilarating sense of the vast future that lay ahead.

I know my father harbors pride for me, yet I cannot predict what the fates may decree. He may one day feel shame for my choices, disown me, or worse. Nevertheless, retreat is not an option; I have pledged my loyalty to the departed, and I shall uphold those vows until my final breath. Taking a deep breath, I offered my heartfelt homage at the feet of the Dargah Ajmer Sharif.

Astawdi,' "ullaaha deenaka wa amaanataka, wa khawaateema 'amalik."

"Shukran Awais, do come to Dubai. It would be an honor to host you in my home." Awais Omar, a scholar from Dubai University, embodied a God-fearing spirit and was delightful company.

"Allah Karim, Bhai jaan," his little sister burst in to bid farewell. "Bhai Jaan, I've packed a few things for Tabeeya Baji, Imtiyaz Bhai jaan, and Abu."

"Thank you, Ruwaha," I replied with a warm wave. The sweet girl, so innocent and joyful, reminded everyone around her of love, positivity, and laughter.

Over the years, Awais and his family had woven themselves into the fabric of our lives in India. He had chosen to drive me personally to Delhi.

As we journeyed down the highway, gazing out the window, nostalgia washed over me, bringing forth memories of my family's arduous journey; from Pakistan to Dubai, it had been a long and challenging path. My grandfather's monumental decision to leave behind everything to forge a new existence was not taken lightly. Each year, my father steadfastly maintained the tradition of visiting Ajmer Sharif, our ancestral home before the partition. I recall my grandfather recounting tales of those times, lamenting that the separation was both cruel and unwarranted.

The drive from Ajmer to Delhi stretched on, yet I hardly dared to blink, for I had yearned and prayed for this moment for years.

"Allah hafiz! Awais, until we meet again," I said, embracing him for a few lingering seconds.

"India to Dubai Emirates passenger report to gate no 2."

It had been six moons since the fateful day, when the chilling headline "Taj Express Car Crash Kills Two," echoed through the pages. Just six words, yet they shattered my universe. In their wake, I was left adrift in a sea of memories; for countless days, I wandered, lost to the world beyond my sorrow.

Dad was my steadfast anchor, while Mom was the vessel that navigated life's tumultuous waters. In their absence, I felt as though I were sinking beneath the waves. They were my confidants, my sages, my guiding stars. Dad regaled me with his most treasured tales after a few sips of courage—his life's heartaches and awe-inspiring adventures, often revolving around Mom. As for her, she was my moral compass, embodying purity and a fierce sense of justice. Draped in elegance, she moved with a grace that enchanted all who beheld her. I often pondered how many admirers had sought to capture her heart before Dad won her over.

They entrusted Vinayak, Kaashvi, and me to navigate the labyrinth of life's harshest truths alone. The sweetest refuge for a child lies in the embrace of their parents, shielded from the tumult of the outside world.

In those tender moments when the clock struck 6 a.m., and Mom gently roused me for homework, I would often smile in sleepy defiance, hoping to steal a few precious minutes of slumber. Her loving fingers would weave through my hair, bestowing blessings for the day ahead, invoking the divine to safeguard my journey. With a curious heart, she would inquire about my dreams, skillfully coaxing me from the embrace of sleep, all without my full awareness of the magic at play.

I nestled into my spacious seat, fidgeting with my fingers in a dance of anxious anticipation. A glance out the window revealed the magnificent evening sky of Delhi, a canvas painted with countless memories. I watched the distant ballet of planes, the trucks laden with luggage, and the diligent souls braving the elements. In that moment of stillness, a wave of nostalgia washed over me; my heart ached with the thought of missing the sunrise, the sweet fragrance of morning blooms, the bustling traffic, the tantalizing flavors of my homeland, and all that brought me joy. Each cherished memory whispered echoes of my parents, resonating deeply within.

I sighed! The icy grip of the handle on my seat tugged me back to reality, a weight settling upon my heart. I was on the brink of tears, a tempest within me. Drawing in a deep breath, I valiantly attempted to stave off the flood, yet it was in vain; tears cascaded down my cheeks, igniting my cheeks with warmth and turning them crimson. I could truly feel the crimson rivulets traced paths down my face. With trembling hands, I wiped my tears upon my mother's cherished scarf; feeling utterly shattered, I clutched it tighter against my heart. In that moment of solitude, I grasped the weight of my choice to depart this land. Yet, I could not linger in the very home that held countless cherished memories with my beloved parents without their spirits haunting my thoughts.

Their souls would ache to witness my fragility, a sight I could not bear to inflict upon them.

The choice to embark on a new chapter in Dubai weighed heavily on my heart; all I possessed was a glimmer of "hope." I yearned for Dubai to embrace me!

Peering through the window at the twinkling airport lights, I craved tranquility, seeking solace to soothe the storm swirling within. The ache of missing them was profound, and I could no longer contain my emotions. "Ma'am, is everything all right?" A flight attendant inquired gently, her hand resting on my shoulder, concern etched upon her face.

As I turned to meet her gaze, I became aware of the tears cascading down my cheeks, the sobs echoing louder than I had imagined.

Oh no, this moment couldn't have been more mortifying. The flight crew, accompanied by a handful of passengers, encircled me, their eyes brimming with concern. I yearned to wail, yet I mustered a smile in response to their kindness. "Water," was the lone word I could utter. "Of course, ma'am," she replied graciously before departing to fetch it.

As the throngs continued to board the flight, those gathered near my seat offered gentle, reassuring smiles.

The air hostess presented me with a water bottle, her smile radiant and wide, as if it held the secrets of joy itself. I marveled at her ability to maintain such brightness, a gift I had struggled to embrace in recent months. "Can I assist you with anything else, ma'am?" She inquired softly. "No, thank you. I am fine now," I replied, dabbing at the remnants of my tears. "Ma'am, may I kindly request the passenger of this seat to reclaim his place? He has been waiting patiently while you were tended to." "Oh! Yes, please," I responded, a wave of guilt washing over me for the fellow traveler.

I shifted in my seat as a tall, dashing young man, clad in black, settled beside me. His blue eyes sparkled like the sea, yet radiated the warmth of the sun. For a fleeting moment, our gazes intertwined, his eyes silently inquiring if I felt any better. I nodded, offering a gentle smile, my own eyes still glistening, red from tears.

As the plane ascended into the sky, I turned my gaze to the window. The city lights twinkled like stars, illuminating the roads below.

The soup was being served when the flight attendant gently roused me from my slumber. I quietly savored the warmth of my soup, adrift in a sea of contemplation.

My musings were suddenly pierced by the inquiry of my seatmate, Mr. Bluish Black. Indeed, I could aptly name him so, for his striking blue eyes sparkled beneath the shadow of his black suit. "Are you okay?" He whispered, with his slow blinks and curious smile.

I smiled back and nodded, "Better."

He possessed an Arabic accent, yet his essence hinted at Indian roots. "Dewan-e-Ghalib" graced his lap, as his gentle hands caressed the pages with the utmost tenderness, and those enchanting eyes seemed to savor each word. Deeply immersed in the poem, he radiated an aura of familiarity that eluded my grasp. I glanced at him once more, attempting to unravel the mystery of where we had crossed paths, but my thoughts drifted into a realm beyond, leaving me adrift in the void of the flight.

In a quest for tranquility, I reclined in my seat, reminiscing about the moments when Dad would recite Ghalib's verses,

"Ishq se tabiyat ne jist ka mazza paya, Dard ki dava payi, dard ladva paya"

(Love is the cure to anything and everything, but there is no cure for love.)

I was drifting to sleep when I felt the blanket gently settling over me. I just smiled in gratitude, as I had no energy to open my eyes to thank the pretty lady. Exhausted, I drifted off to sleep.

The announcement of landing woke me up; the voice echoed the sounds of belts ticking, bright light falling on the pages of the book my co-passenger was reading. It took me a while to return to my senses and brush my hands on my hair. I grabbed the rubber band from my wrist and tied a high bun. I felt lighter but still was in some haze as if I was just merely passing through the motions but could not handle it. "Can I help you with something?" Mr. Bluish black asked again. "Umm, no, I am good." I showed him the water bottle in my hand.

He closed his book, placed it on his lap, tightened his seat belt, and rested his hands on it. He noticed me staring at him and his actions. "Everything good?" He asked again and caught me gazing at him. "Oh yeah! I just felt like I had seen you somewhere." "Small world," he said, smiling. It was indeed a flawless smile with dimples overpowering the cheeks.

Outside, darkness enveloped the world, yet the city's lights shimmered like stars, illuminating the night as if it were day. The towering skyscrapers left me in a spellbound state, for I had never beheld such a breathtaking panorama view from the sky. As we approached the earth, the roads, parks, traffic signals, and buildings unfurled beneath us.

With a gentle thud, the plane kissed the ground, and the pilot's voice echoed through the cabin, announcing it was safe to unfasten our seatbelts and rise. Mr. Bluish Black stood, pivoting towards me. "Khuda hafiz," he uttered, a smile dancing on his lips as he departed.

CHAPTER 2

As the golden rays of the sun poured through the window, they gently woke me from my sleep. I found myself wrestling with the cozy sheets, wriggling in my bed for a fleeting moment before the realization dawned that I was in the enchanting city of Dubai. Stretching languidly, I gazed up at the ceiling, my mind still lost in dreams. The melodious chirping of birds outside my window made me walk towards it. My room here was more spacious from the one I had back in India. Adorned in soothing shades of blue and lavender, the walls cradled a set of pristine white Croatian curtains, while the room featured a sumptuous double bed. I was particularly enchanted by the charmingly designed side table and the grand wooden almirahs that stood sentinel in the space.

The view outside my window—the vibrant flowers, playful little birds, and blooming palm trees—danced in a kaleidoscope of colors. The architecture of the nearby houses was a tapestry of uniqueness and elegance. With each passing moment, the heat outside intensified, causing the palm fronds in the driveway to sway gracefully in the wind. The rustling leaves serenaded me with their gentle whispers, as the breeze orchestrated its own soothing symphony and a few cars meandered along the road.

Suddenly, I was jolted from my reverie by the ringing of the phone.

"Hello, Di," I greeted Kaashvi's call, who had always embodied a motherly spirit for both Vinayak and me.

"Hi! How was the flight?" She inquired, a hint of concern lacing her voice.

"It was okay!" I managed to reply, though the truth was more complicated.

"I know you cried," she asserted, her tone firm yet caring.

"How do you always know everything?" I stumbled over my words, caught off guard.

"Ah, motherly genes were activated long ago," she replied, a hint of amusement in her voice.

I scoffed, "I am fine now, and how are the little ones?"

"Kids are sleeping. How is the apartment?"

I recognized her gentle nudge, steering the conversation towards the wonders surrounding me.

"It is not an apartment. It's a duplex," I corrected, stepping out of the room, only to be greeted by the grandeur of the residence provided by the company.

I gazed up at the lofty ceiling and exquisite craftsmanship, marveling at every detail of my new sanctuary.

"Hello? Tanisha!" Her voice echoed with concern.

"Yeah, hello! Di, you are going to love this place," I replied, excitement bubbling in my tone. "It is so beautiful," I continued, gliding from the hall into the open kitchen that faced the living room.

"The living room is softly illuminated by vintage wall sconces, with a set of antique couches resting upon a contemporary-style carpet." I admired the colossal window, parting the luxurious plum velvet curtains that harmonized with the cream walls. "A painting with a maroon background adorns one side of the window, inscribed with an Arabic quote, while the opposite wall boasts an antique watch, intricately designed with red Arabic calligraphy. The grand wooden dining table completes this minimal yet classic decor," I declared, utterly enchanted by the ambiance.

"I bet there are secret passages hidden behind the walls," Kaashvi laughed.

"Mom would have adored this place, Kaashvi; everything here reflects her taste: the abundant light, the flowers, the furniture, even the curtains and open kitchen."

"Open kitchen! To keep an eye on us while cooking," she chuckled, then her tone softened, "Tanisha, they are in a better place; keep them in your heart and aim for the skies."

Sensing my melancholy, I pivoted the topic, "How is Vinayak? Is he ok?"

"He is good, don't worry. And don't forget to try those eateries Vinayak suggested; he'll be thrilled to hear you've tasted those kebabs and shawarmas."

"Oh! I will."

"Bye, have fun." And with that, she hung up.

I opened the kitchen drawers in search of coffee, but the stark white drawers and partially filled cupboards stared back at me.

With a steaming cup in hand, I stepped into the garden. The grass felt like a soft embrace beneath my feet. It was tranquil, and for the first time in ages, I felt at peace as I sipped my coffee, watching the birds flit about.

As I wandered further, I noticed the grand gate at the entrance, complete with security alarms, leading to the driveway that graced the porch.

With a day before I joined the office and only a casual meeting scheduled, I glanced at my phone, noting I had time to indulge in the famous breakfast Vinayak had recommended.

The daunting task of "unpacking" awaited me. I pulled out the first item my hand grasped from the depths of my suitcase. Scoffing at the black pencil skirt, I dove back in to search for my white shirt.

Glancing in the mirror, I admired how the outfit flattered my figure. A messy bun seemed the wisest choice, keeping me cool in the scorching heat while still looking elegant.

Stepping outside, I felt the warmth envelop me, Vinayak's warnings about Dubai's heat echoing in my mind as he extolled its vibrant lifestyle and car clubs, transforming into my personal encyclopedia of all things Dubai.

As the cab arrived, a man in his early 40s opened the door for me, greeting me with a warm smile, "Salam Alaikum."

"Walikuma Aslam," I returned the greeting, feeling the warmth of his demeanor.

He repeated the destination, "Al Ustad Special Kebab, near Al Fahidi Metro Station," before we set off.

"Are you sightseeing?" He asked in a cheerful tone.

"No!" I replied, minimizing my response, fearing I was impolite.

"You're not from Dubai?" I ventured, attempting to soften my abruptness.

"I'm from Afghanistan! I came here when I was 22, and it's been my home for 20 years," he shared, his voice laced with a hint of nostalgia.

As he recounted his journey to Dubai, the challenges of convincing his parents, and his rise from laborer to established transport business owner, I gazed out the window, captivated by the vibrant life beyond.

"Is there no traffic at this hour?" I inquired, hoping to steer the conversation.

"The traffic is well-managed, Bibi; computers control the lights and divert traffic for a smooth flow. The laws here are strict, with hefty fines," he continued, unabated.

"Where are you from, Bibi?" He asked, glancing at me through the rearview mirror.

"India," I replied, checking the time and directions on my phone.

"India! A beautiful country. I dream of visiting the Taj Mahal and Hazrat Nizamuddin Dargah one day," he said, his eyes sparkling with enthusiasm.

"Is this your first time in Dubai?" He asked, stopping at a red light.

"Yes," I responded, marveling at the colorful tapestry of cultures and beautifully adorned cafes passing by.

He made a slow right turn, "Al Ustad Special Kebab is here."

As I fished for dirhams, 100-rupee note in my wallet took me back in time and nostalgia washed over me; I will miss bargaining with the auto drivers in India.

Snapping back to reality, I rummaged through my purse for dirhams, handing over 20, twice what I would have paid back in Delhi for a ride.

"Khuda Hafiz," he said, waving as he drove away.

Walking a few steps down the bustling lane, the enticing aromas of spices enveloped me as I entered the grand glass door of the restaurant. The rustic wooden décor enchanted me: money plants in tiny ceramic pots, the gentle glow from scented candles on each table, linen runners, and jute mats perfectly aligned with the café's aesthetic.

I chose a table by the glass window, overlooking the lively street filled with honking cars and bustling pedestrians. The menu offered a plethora of dishes: Iranian kebabs, Chelo Kebabs, Emirati pancakes, and 'Al Machboos,' a fragrant chicken rice dish. After 15 minutes of delightful deliberation, I settled on Persian kebabs and Emirati Pancakes to satisfy my sweet tooth.

As I waited, I admired the walls adorned with photos of famous visitors and an eclectic display of world currencies. When my food arrived, the kebabs, garnished with colorful salad and seasonings, paired with crispy fries, melted in my mouth with the first bite. The smoky flavor from the charcoal grill danced beautifully with the raw onions and grilled tomatoes accompanying the kebabs.

The golden Emirati pancakes, infused with cardamom and saffron, drizzled with date syrup and topped with silvered pistachios, were nothing short of heavenly. The restaurant buzzed with patrons coming and going. After settling the bill and checking the time, I realized I was late for my first day at the office.

I swiftly booked another cab and hurriedly departed for the day ahead.

CHAPTER 3

"Saif Sahib will arrive shortly; please, make yourself at ease, Irtaka Bhai Jaan," the house attendant warmly ushered him to the sitting area.

As Irtaka settled into the familiar space, memories of his childhood danced through his mind—days spent studying the Quran and reciting hymns he had memorized. He recalled how Saif Sahib had always showered him with affection for his quick wit and keen learning, but today, a whisper of fear lingered in his heart. What if his teacher disagreed with him?

"Irtaka! Subhaan Allah! What brings you here, my child? Come, let us share breakfast." Saif Sahib beckoned, leading the way to the dining table.

Following closely, Irtaka noted the same long strides that Saif Sahib took, his tailored suit—a masterpiece from the finest tailors—still impeccably crafted just as it had been in his youth. Each crease was perfectly pressed, the fabric draped with precision. His hair remained flawless, and the gentle aroma of his essence enveloped him. Every detail, from the decor to the delicacies on his plate, reflected his elegance.

As Saif Sahib settled into his chair, he smiled warmly at Irtaka, serving him a plate of Liquimat. The moment Irtaka savored the Liquimat and —he felt the warmth of Saif Sahib's affection.

Irtaka knew that if he could win over Saif Sahib, he could sway anyone in the upcoming meeting.

"What troubles you?" Saif Sahib inquired, gazing into Irtaka's eyes.

Gathering his courage, Irtaka declared, "Will you support a decision I wish to propose for the company?"

"Child, you have elevated the company to new heights. What makes you hesitate?" Saif Sahib responded, a hint of concern in his voice.

"I plan to expand our operations by opening a new branch in Abu Dhabi, to gradually establish a solid foundation there," Irtaka replied, conviction lending strength to his words.

"Mashallah Alhamdulillah... Alhumdillah!" Saif Sahib beamed with delight.

"Thus, I summoned an urgent Board meeting and came to fetch you for the office personally," he added with a gentle smile.

"Child, I have known you since you were little," Saif Sahib continued, placing his spoon down. "I can sense there's more to your visit than this," he remarked with calm assurance.

Irtaka met his teacher's gaze, knowing that hiding anything from him was in vain. "I want to hire a girl for Ibrahim's position!" He stated, awaiting his response, only to find Saif Sahib momentarily speechless.

"A girl?" He echoed in disbelief. "Ji!"

"And Ibrahim?" Saif Sahib's gaze questioned him further. "He will transition to the position in Abu Dhabi," Irtaka replied, his resolve unwavering. "As you see fit!" He added, his smile tinged with uncertainty.

As I walked through the large halls, memories of my first job resurfaced. I recalled how my mother, more anxious than I, had taken a day off to accompany me to the interview, earning me the endearing title of 'Mum's girl'—forever treated as a child.

Entering a narrow passage, I was struck by the décor that echoed my own workplace. As I approached the open area, a woman greeted me with a radiant smile. I found myself captivated by her beauty; her warm smile was inviting, and the hijab framing her oval face was perfectly styled, revealing just enough of her features. The eyeliner accentuated her hazel eyes, which sparkled with a calming innocence reminiscent of a child.

"How may I assist you?" She inquired, her voice a gentle caress.

Lost in my thoughts, I stammered, "Umm, Mr. Ibrahim, yes, Mr. Ibrahim Siddique, I have a meeting with him."

She regarded me with warmth and replied, "You must be Miss Tanisha Oberoi." I nodded in affirmation, a smile flickering across my face.

As we exchanged smiles, she guided me to the waiting area, offering water while I observed her every graceful movement. She handled everything with the tenderness of a rose petal, and the warmth of her spirit radiated from her glowing visage. "You can call me Alia. Mr. Ibrahim will be with you shortly; please let me know if you need anything else."

Moments later, my name echoed from across the room, jolting me upright. I turned towards the familiar voice and saw a man approaching, with broad smile.

"Good afternoon! It is a pleasure to have you here," he greeted, his expressions wide and inviting.

"Same here," I replied, returning his smile.

"I am Ibrahim Siddique; I have been conducting your interview calls," he said briskly.

Ah, that explained the familiarity! His Arabic accent, the melancholic timbre of his voice, and his command of every note made it resonate like a beautiful melody. I couldn't help but wonder what a splendid singer he must be.

"How was your journey?" He inquired, breaking the brief silence.

"Comfortable," I responded, smiling once more.

"There is something important we need to discuss," he continued, his tone shifting to one of palpable excitement as he offered me a seat and settled across the table.

"Since you are appointed to a challenging position, we would like you to start today; thus, the 'management' wishes to meet you in person," he stated, awaiting my response. My heart skipped a beat.

He held my resume, appointment letter, and other credentials, declaring, "NOW!"

"NOW!" I echoed, a touch louder than intended. The word sent shivers cascading down my spine; twisting my stomach, and surging my anxiety to new heights..

"Yes, right now!" He affirmed with a reassuring smile, noticing my shock. I managed to smile in return, attempting to mask my swirling emotions. Mr. Ibrahim appeared so composed and relaxed, as unruffled as his impeccably ironed attire. I pondered whether he had ever felt panic in his life.

He gestured for me to follow, and I did so quietly, thoughts swirling in my mind like arrows. My breath quickened for two reasons: this was a far cry from what I had envisioned for my first day! Moreover, I had to mini-jog to keep pace with his long strides.

How does one greet in Dubai? My thoughts felt scattered, as if I had lost my voice and clarity, my mind blank like a canvas before an exam. I had perused the website, yet the information eluded me now.

"It will all be fine!" Mr. Ibrahim reassured me, sensing my adrenaline spiking like a seasoned guide. I smiled back, striving to keep up with him.

As we stood before the grand entrance of the conference room, I beheld a large rectangular table set horizontally, accommodating four individuals engrossed in conversation, deliberation, and document review.

Mr. Ibrahim rapped gently on the door, and we glided into the room. I emanated an air of sophistication and grace as I extended my greetings to each esteemed gentleman present.

The first man, positioned on the far left, was in his fifties, adorned in a keffiyeh, Igal, and bhist. His countenance radiated a serene tranquility, while the rosary in his hand swayed gently, his fingers gliding over the beads in a rhythmic dance of devotion. God's name flowed melodiously from his lips, and his mere presence felt like a blessing; it was as if he had fulfilled his earthly duties, offering gratitude for every divine bounty bestowed upon him. A soothing wave of calm enveloped me at the sight of him; he was Mohammed Bin Ali Al Abbar, a figure I recognized from the official website. He had dedicated his life to serving the royals of Dubai, infusing his visionary spirit to a progressive Dubai.

As my gaze shifted to the next individual, I noted his formal attire, reminiscent of my father's generation. He greeted me with a warm, reassuring smile. This was Raad Mohammed, a distinguished professor from Dubai University and a revered literary scholar. I had perused several of his articles while assisting my mother, and I learned he had also represented the UN in his earlier years.

The third figure was Saif Ahmad Al Ghurair, a kindred spirit in age. His visage bore an air of stoicism, as though engaged in a silent debate, yet upon meeting my gaze, he smiled and settled more comfortably into his seat.

What held my eyes was the fourth person, those bluish eyes and black suit. Our eyes met, and I felt betrayed by my mind. Why didn't I recognize him yesterday? Mr. Irtaka Haider, a board member, was right next to me on the plane. The person was sitting next to me the whole fucking time, and I did not recognize him. I knew it; his face did seem familiar from the website, and I could not recall it. This wasn't very comfortable; I could see him mockingly smile at me. He was enjoying it, but I knew I had to grin back for now.

"Small World," I scoffed under my breath. "Good morning!" I said loud enough to be audible.

"Please have a seat, Miss Tanisha Oberoi, and welcome to Dubai," he said merrily, enjoying the act.

"With your esteemed appointment as General Manager of the new branch, Mr. Ibrahim, the board has resolved that our endeavors in Abu Dhabi shall commence this very week." He paused, casting a meaningful glance towards Mr. Ibrahim.

"Yes, Sayidi Almuhtarm!" Mr. Ibrahim replied, his tone imbued with solemnity.

"We eagerly anticipate your ascension of the business and new office to dazzling new heights," Raad

Mohammed proclaimed, "And for the record, the financials have been meticulously managed."

Mr. Ibrahim's smile was wide, and I could almost hear his inner joy echoing like a joyous hula hoop, yet what was Almutram?

Mohammed Bin Ali Al Abbar and Saif Ahmed Al Ghurair remained silent, their smiles radiating warmth as they nodded in polite agreement.

"Miss Tanisha," Mr. Irtaka began, his tone laced with a hint of challenge, "We trust you are prepared to embrace this opportunity. I shall oversee your progress directly.

I am determined to become a valuable asset to the company in no time," I replied with newfound confidence.

"We eagerly anticipate that," he retorted, a smirk dancing upon his lips.

The room felt lighter after I had spoken up. It was as if someone had just boosted my confidence.

Mr. Ibrahim rose to his feet, and I followed suit, struggling to grasp the nuances of the conversation, ensnared by the unfamiliar accent and vocabulary.

As we ascended, Mr. Irtaka's gaze was a focused and anchoring me in place. Our eyes locked, and in that moment, a spark of excitement danced within him, as if he had achieved a significant milestone. The company's expansion loomed large, casting a hopeful glow, I guess.

I trailed behind Mr. Ibrahim to his office, where he graciously offered me a seat and wished me well. A gentle knock disrupted the moment, revealing Alia, holding files. She placed them on the table, graced me with a warm smile, and departed as Mr. Ibrahim excused himself.

Alone in his office, I marveled at the artistry that adorned the space. Mr. Ibrahim's eye for perfection was evident in his antique collections and exquisite artifacts. Every file was meticulously labeled, and even the stationery found its rightful place; it was clear he was a true perfectionist.

"How was the journey?" Mr. Irtaka's voice startled me from behind. I turned, seeking support from the sturdy desk.

"I apologize for the fright," he said, his tone lowered with sincerity.

"No, I'm fine. I thought I was alone."

"Mr. Ibrahim?" I inquired.

"Oh yes! He's in his cabin."

I glanced around, realizing I was in Mr. Irtaka's office.

"How are you today?" He continued.

"I'm well, and the flight was pleasant." I hesitated, pondering why he hadn't revealed his identity the day prior; perhaps he too was unfamiliar with me.

Engrossed in his phone, he seemed oblivious as I admired the rich decor enveloping us. His office boasted solid tapestries and intricate wooden craftsmanship. My mother would have reveled in the authentic metal artifacts; it was clear he possessed a passion for art.

Moments later, Mr. Ibrahim returned, announcing, "I'll show you your cabin and introduce you to the office staff." I stole a glance at Mr. Irtaka, still tethered to his device, before standing to follow Mr. Ibrahim.

We walked to the main hall, where the spacious work areas awaited. To call them mere cubicles would be a disservice; the ambiance rivaled that of a five-star hotel, with soft mirrors and carefully curated lighting illuminating the space, exuding a regal charm. I gazed around, feeling like a child lost in a land of wonder.

A woman in her early forties approached, extending her hand for a handshake—a gesture not commonly practiced in Dubai, but times were changing. I grasped her hand firmly as she smiled.

"Almusafahat hi daghdagha." She laughed, retracting her hand. I glanced at Mr. Ibrahim for a translation. "She finds handshakes ticklish," he replied with a chuckle.

I found myself caught in a whirlwind of emotions, laughter and tears intertwining like delicate threads. Before I could fully grasp this tumult, I stepped forward and embraced her, feeling an aching longing for my mother, stronger than ever in that moment.

Smiles blossomed around me, welcoming me to this new journey.

As I turned back, Alia awaited me, with her warm smile.

"Miss Tanisha, allow me to guide you to your cabin and introduce you to everyone," she offered with a friendly smile.

With that, she led me through the bustling office to a corner where a glass door stood ajar. Upon entering, I entered a spacious L-shaped cabin adorned with elegant dark brown furniture and a polished wooden floor. Yet, before I could fully immerse myself in this luxurious haven, my gaze fell upon the sign "IT" elegantly engraved on the glass-covered table.

"What does this sign mean? Is it the company's logo?" I inquired, my tone laced with curiosity.

"IT stands for Mr. Irtaka's logo; he believes it brings him good fortune," Alia replied, a glimmer of amusement dancing in her eyes.

As she explained the various passwords, emails, and documents I would need, I found my mind drifting, distracted by the wonders surrounding me. Perhaps it was jet lag or hunger that dulled my senses, for I scarcely absorbed her words. Noticing my distraction, she smiled patiently, waiting for me to return from my reverie.

"I'll gather the essentials for you and handle other requirements," she said, gracefully leaving me to my thoughts.

"Thank you," I replied, appreciating her thoughtfulness. She struck me as exceptionally bright.

Gazing out the window, I marveled at the dusky sunlight and the bustling traffic below. Inside, however, there was a serene silence, as if I were witnessing life from a great distance.

After about an hour, Alia knocked gently at my door. I was astonished to realize how quickly time had flown while I sat lost in contemplation.

I smiled and gestured for her to enter, enveloped in a haze of disbelief, feeling as if I were suspended in a dream, teetering between reality and an aching past. The weight of my sorrow felt so familiar that happiness seemed like a distant fantasy.

"Mr. Irtaka would like to see you in his office," she informed me, placing some files upon the table before exiting.

As I made my way to his cabin, I noticed colleagues leaving the office.

"Miss Tanisha, we have a presentation to prepare," he said, eyes glued to his laptop screen.

"What is its focus?" I asked, curiosity piqued.

"It concerns the market strategy you outlined during your interview, where you articulated compelling reasons for our private firm to partner with government projects, thereby ushering in a new architectural revolution. Your fundraising techniques were particularly noteworthy," he said, his gaze unwavering.

His Arabic accent was melodic, though certain words like "collaborators" and "government" made me smile inwardly.

"That was merely an interview, Mr. Irtaka!" I protested.

"But those ideas originated from you, did they not?" He replied, an eyebrow raised, prompting astonishment to wash over me.

"Yes, Mr. Irtaka, they were indeed my ideas, though I may require more details to finalize the presentation," I admitted, slightly irked.

"Of course! Whatever you need," he said, sliding his laptop toward me.

Taking a deep breath, I settled into the chair and opened the device. As the screen lit up, the familiar "IT" logo appeared, prompting me to glance curiously at him.

"Do you require something, Miss Tanisha?" He inquired.

"Yes, the password for the laptop, please."

He leaned closer, the space between us narrowing as he typed swiftly.

His presence was intoxicating, his cologne enveloping me like a warm embrace. I realized then why perfume commercials felt so relatable. Noticing my reaction, I shyly turned away.

"I have a few questions regarding the presentation," I ventured to ease the tension. "Please, go ahead!" He encouraged, his tone lowering as he stepped aside.

"Are we focusing solely on government companies for partnerships, or will we also consider private companies? If we do, who will we approach first? Which sectors are most profitable for our firm? Will collaborations with the private sector be project-based or annual?" I asked in one breath.

"Those are a great many questions, Miss Tanisha," he chuckled.

I felt my cheeks flush, realizing how foolish I acted in enthusiasm.

"Allah Mehram!" He exclaimed, pausing to gather his thoughts before sitting down.

"We will collaborate on government-owned projects alongside private players. The builders we engage with have played significant roles in constructing the Burj

Khalifa. They find our projects and innovative ideas appealing and wish to merge with us officially, benefiting from timely services and striking architecture."

"Our partnerships will afford us government subsidies and connections throughout the UAE. They will serve as shadow partners initially, but they will stand by us, as the union of government and private enterprises will solidify our status as established builders in the UAE, paving the way for numerous governments, semi-government, and private projects," he concluded, tucking a pen into his shirt pocket.

My jaw dropped, completely taken aback by the magnitude of what he was saying. I had anticipated a mundane meeting with administrative officials, merely discussing the company's progress over coffee. Yet here I was, poised to create a presentation for some of the world's leading architects. It was overwhelming.

"Are you alright?" He asked with a hint of sarcasm.

"Don't worry; I have faith in your abilities."

I Stared at him, and was a little speechless. But as I engaged in a deeper discussion about the presentation, we lost track of time and just then, my phone rang, and I instantly knew who it was. Before answering, I glanced at Mr. Irtaka, indicating the urgency.

He turned to gaze out the window as I picked up the call.

"Hello, Di!" I said, my voice tinged with panic.

"Hi, where are you, and what have you eaten?" She asked, concern evident in her tone.

"I'm sorry, I'm a bit busy. Can I call you back?" I hurriedly replied, trying to cut the conversation short.

"What? You had no plans today! Where are you?" Her voice rose, "Did you eat anything?"

"No, I'll be home soon and will call you back," I insisted, desperate to end the call.

"Seriously, you haven't eaten? If that's why you didn't want me to come with you, wait! I'm booking the next flight to Dubai!" My sister's voice boomed, drawing attention and making me cringe in embarrassment.

"Kaashvi, please! I'll grab a bite and message you, but I'm busy right now. I'll call you after I eat," I said firmly, hoping she would understand. "Bye," I added, hanging up, mortified by her treatment of me.

"Was that your sister?" He asked, curiosity dancing in his eyes.

"Yes, my elder sister," I replied, attempting to regain composure. "Oh, but she's right," he noted, concern etching his features.

I looked at him, wondering if he had overheard my entire conversation. "So, you haven't eaten anything?" He pressed, shifting the topic. "I'm not familiar with many places, and it has been a hectic day!" I replied, infusing a hint of sarcasm into my tone.

"I'm hungry too; would you care to join me for dinner?" He proposed, his voice uncertain as he gauged my reaction.

"Sure," I replied, though a pang of apprehension gripped me at the thought of dining with him.

As we stepped outside, I was captivated by Dubai's vibrant nightlife. It was 10:30 PM, and the streets sparkled with pools of white light. Being in an industrial area, the towering buildings appeared to kiss the sky, and luxurious cars lined the streets. "What would you like to eat?" He asked, leading me toward the car.

"Food," I replied, pausing, my stomach rumbling in agreement.

As we sped down the highway in his Lamborghini, the car suddenly veered right, the tires screeched, and I found myself tumbling against his shoulder. Instinctively, I clutched him tightly to steady myself.

"Irtaka!" I exclaimed, startled.

He swiftly hit the brakes, regaining control. It dawned on me that it was merely a sharp turn in his luxurious, adrenaline-fueled vehicle. I berated myself for my reaction, slowly releasing my grip and retreating to my seat. An awkward silence enveloped us.

"I apologize," he broke the quiet. "It was a hasty decision, and I had to take that sharp turn."

"I'm sorry too!" I replied, feeling the heat rise to my cheeks.

He parked outside Jam Base, one of Dubai's finest restaurants. The ambiance was enchanting, illuminated by soft yellow lights and adorned with rich wooden interiors. As we entered, I noticed a diverse crowd—tourists and the elite of Dubai mingling together. Women donned Abayas, the national attire, while the men sported Kanduras. My preconceived notions of Dubai as a rigidly traditional place were slowly melting away; here, people wore a blend of styles, from traditional to casual.

As we glided toward the table, I sensed curious gazes upon us; my fair skin gradually flushed crimson, a wave of discomfort washing over me. It was my inaugural day at work, and here I was, sharing a late-night meal with my boss—a moment tinged with awkwardness. The weight of those stares urged me to shift uneasily in my chair, acutely aware of their scrutiny. I glanced at him, my eyes brimming with silent questions, and he responded with a warm smile.

"It's because of me; here, most are friends or family, and they've never witnessed me socializing. Would you prefer to go somewhere else?" He inquired kindly.

"Umm, no, all good," I replied, though restlessness simmered beneath my calm façade.

A fleeting silence enveloped us, as time itself seemed to pause—the air, the gestures, the very essence of our interaction hung in stillness.

"Why is that?" I finally mustered the courage to break the hush.

"Why is what?" His Arabic accent danced around his words.

"Why don't you socialize?" I hesitated but pressed on!

"Never felt inclined to," he replied, his gaze piercing into mine for a lingering moment. Just then, the waiter interrupted, "Sir, your order!"

I turned to the waiter, then cast my eyes around the dimly lit room. The atmosphere thickened, a palpable tension filling the space, and my heart raced as if it were gasping for breath. The clinks of cutlery accentuated the heavy silence. As the waiter arranged our meals, I found myself lost in thought, overwhelmed by new, intoxicating sensations swirling within me. I could feel Mr. Irtaka's gaze; our eyes would occasionally collide, prompting me to retreat back to my plate. My appetite had vanished, yet I continued to eat—an ultimate distraction from the awkwardness and lingering eye contact.

"Can I ask you something?" I ventured, looking up at him.

"Please," he set his spoon aside, giving me his full attention.

"Did you know who I was on the flight yesterday?" I inquired softly, seeking the depths of his eyes. "Yes, I was aware," he replied.

"Then why did you not say anything?" My voice grew firmer, curiosity igniting within me.

"You appeared upset, Miss Tanisha!"

"But how did you recognize me?" I asked, bewildered.

"Miss Tanisha, I hired you," he answered with a hint of a smirk.

"Then why not acknowledge me?" I pressed.

"Goodbyes are rarely simple; I thought you needed your space," he replied, resuming his meal.

"Thank you," I said, offering a weary smile.

"Why?" He queried, lifting his gaze.

"Dinner!" I replied, .

He smiled and mouthed a silent, "Thank you."

I smiled back, immersing myself in my food. There was an enigmatic aura about Irtaka, layered and complex. I sensed warmth, yet the mystery enveloped him, leaving me with a flurry of questions begging to be answered.

CHAPTER 4

Alia neatly folded her mat after Namaz, hastening towards the kitchen to assist Tabeeya, who was already weary from her tasks.

"Baji, please sit; you should not be exerting yourself in this condition," she urged with genuine concern.

"I am merely preparing tea; could you hand me some milk?"

"You are pregnant, Baji. You need to rest," she smiled, passing her the milk carton.

"Is everything well at the office?" Tabeeya asked, a hint of worry lacing her voice.

"Ji Baji, why do you ask?" Alia paused, meeting Tabeeya's gaze.

"Your Bhai Jaan came home very late yesterday and skipped dinner," Tabeeya replied, her voice tinged with concern.

"He must have been busy preparing for the presentation," Alia responded, handing Tabeeya a bottle of coconut water.

"Baji, doesn't it hurt to know he hasn't fully accepted you?"

"He regards me as a family member; for now, that is enough," Alia replied with calm assurance. "Baji, do you think this baby will change him?" She inquired, standing still.

"I pray he feels differently when he cradles the baby in his arms."

Tabeeya had joined the household two years ago, pouring her heart into every task and every family member. She embodied love and patience, a giver even when her kindness was not reciprocated. Her tireless efforts had forged her into a strong, independent woman, skillfully balancing her business while embracing the roles of a devoted wife and compassionate daughter-in-law.

Tabeeya was a woman of faith, unwavering in her commitment to the family; she never questioned Irtaka's behavior, believing that one day he would come to understand her heart.

"Alia," Raad Mohammad called, asking her to sit beside him.

Alia moved towards the garden, tea tray in hand, while Tabeeya glided gracefully over the soft green grass, flanked by small bonsai trees in wooden boxes on one side and vibrant flower beds on the other.

"Where is Irtaka?" Abu inquired, glancing at Alia, expecting her to know since she was his secretary.

"Abu, I'm heading to the Mosque," Irtaka replied, lightly touching his shoulder and kissing his forehead.

"Breakfast?" Abu asked, concern etched on his face.

"Abu, I'll eat at the office." Irtaka said, turning to leave.
"How is work, Irtaka?" Abu asked, sipping his tea.

"It's quite taxing, Abu, but Alia is a tremendous help." He smiled briefly, then departed without pause.

—⋀—

Kaashvi and I were deep in conversation over the phone as I sipped my coffee, recounting the events of my first day at the office.

"Kaashvi, the city is so vibrant compared to our history books! How is it possible that Mom was a history professor and never visited Dubai? Had she come here, she would have adored it."

Did you really hug the lady in the middle of the office!" She teased.

"She probably thinks I'm a weirdo. Please don't mention it to Vinayak; he'll tease me about it forever," I pleaded and we both laughed

"Oh, he definitely will!" By the way, you have plenty of time; go shopping and explore the city. How's your boss? What's his name again?

Irtaka! Mr. Irtaka Ali Khan."

"Is he handsome?" She asked with excitement.

"Oh! Okay, bye, I'm off to explore the city," I said, sidestepping the topic of my attractive boss.

"You might enjoy exploring people too," she teased.

"Tanisha! Are you enjoying it there?"

"Yes, and I will be fine, don't worry."

"Send me pictures and call Vinayak later. Bye."

"Bye!" I hung up, enveloped in a moment of silence. Deep breath and dressed for the office, planning to visit the "AlFarooq Omar Bin AlKhattab" Mosque, a place I had longed to see and pay my respects. Clad in a light pink Chikankari salwar kameez and a white beaded dupatta adorned with dark pink lace, a birthday gift from Mom.

Upon arriving at the mosque, I was awestruck by its majestic architecture. Colorful tiles framed a traditional fountain, while the opulent cream walls and expansive glass windows shimmered in the sunlight.

As I entered, my gaze was drawn to the towering minarets embellished with glass, bars, and shimmering domes. The tranquility of the place resonated within me, replenishing my spirit. The chandelier, crafted from delicate cut glass, captivated my attention—its brilliance seemed to illuminate the entire space. The intricate craftsmanship of the alabaster marble left me spellbound. As I stepped onto the soft red carpet, it felt heavenly beneath my feet, prompting me to slow my pace and savor each moment.

Seated in a quiet corner with folded hands and closed eyes, I offered thanks to God for the beautiful life unfolding before me. In that moment, I felt no remorse or pain, only gratitude. I prayed for the well-being of my loved ones, asking the omnipresent to remain by my side. Though I missed mom and dad, a flicker of determination ignited within me; this was my time to make them proud.

It was then that I felt a rosary in my hand. Opening my eyes, I saw an elderly lady smiling radiantly at me, her face aglow as if illuminated by a divine light. I gratefully accepted the rosary, and she placed her hands on my head, sending a shiver down my spine. It felt as though an angel had touched me, reassuring me that I was being watched over.

I examined the rosary, each bead inscribed with 'Allah.' Receiving it in this manner felt like a harbinger of good fortune, so I clutched it tightly and closed my eyes again.

As I entered my cabin, my eyes fell upon the sign "IT." It was comforting to see something that resonated with Mr. Irtaka's essence; he seemed too sensible to flaunt his vulnerabilities. I pondered for a moment what IT might signify when Alia's presence at the door drew my attention away.

Alia entered; her expression vibrant as she prepared to share her insights. "Since you'll be working with Mr. Irtaka and don't know him well, let me enlighten you about his nature. He is strict yet possesses a soft heart; he helps others and is very generous. However, he prefers solitude and rarely socializes; people have yet to spot him enjoying outings with friends as he is a true workaholic." Her smile radiated warmth as she recounted this.

As I listened to Alia speak about Irtaka, I sensed her familiarity with him and the affection in her tone. I wanted her to continue, captivated by this other side of my boss, yet I had to interject.

"Alia!" I said, my tone firm yet gentle.

She looked at me, a smile flickering across her face, acknowledging her moment of excitement. "I'll fetch the briefing from Mr. Ibrahim for you," she replied, hurrying out.

Her blend of intelligence and adorableness instantly endeared her to me; her innocent warmth was refreshing.

"Thank you," I said..

I recognized that Alia and I held different views about Mr. Irtaka; he did socialize, and yes, he did enjoy dinner—like the one we had shared the previous night. He did smile, but Alia need not know of that.

Settling into my chair, I tapped my fingers, contemplating where to begin.

CHAPTER 5

It had been nearly a month since I embarked on my new journey at work; Mr. Ibrahim had departed, leaving me to delve into the labyrinth of files that surrounded me. Kaashvi and Vinayak seemed to breathe easier, their worries for me gradually fading. Each morning, I arrived at the office early, drawn by a lack of distractions at home, and lingered late to escape the solitude of my four walls. My office cabin was a sanctuary, offering a blissful panorama of the city and the mesmerizing hues of sunset. In this haven, I seized the extra time to connect with my colleagues. Mrs. Rashida, a warm-hearted woman in her 40s, delighted me with her home-cooked baklava and authentic dishes. Her husband, Mr. Dalia, was my Arabic tutor, guiding me through the intricacies of the language. Though I stumbled over pronunciations, I managed to memorize the Arabic alphabet, discovering that greetings were simple yet nuanced—"Ahlan" for hello.

In English, "How are you?" is universal, but in Arabic, it shifts with gender! *Ezai Hadritak* is for men, while *Ezai Hadritek* is for women—akin to "ka" for men and "ki" for women; a relaxed version I found relatable.

Standing by the glass window, file in hand, a pen tucked in my high-tied bun, I was startled by a knock at the door.

What brings him here? My mind raced as I raised an eyebrow in thought. Navigating the presence of Mr. Irtaka was a challenge; he stirred a flutter of butterflies within me. His solidly built, muscular frame was evident through his white, translucent shirt, sending chills down my spine. His calm demeanor, glowing visage, and radiant aura drew me in like a moth to a flame. Messy yet combed hair and deep, beady eyes worked their magic, while his gentle demeanor combined with maturity held me captive, making the world around me fade away.

He stepped into my cabin, and I noticed the curious glances from others. Yes, whispers filled the office, speculating about the chemistry between us, but I rolled my eyes at the thought. Khalid, the office boy, followed him with two steaming cups of coffee. Surprised, I remained silent, opting to simply pick up a cup.

"Coffee is perfect, just the way I like it. Shukran, Khalid." He typically smiled, but Khalid stood in awe, eyes glued to Mr. Irtaka.

"You needed something?" I asked, eager to rescue Khalid from his spell. "Umm, yes," he replied, uncertainty lacing his tone.

"You could have called me." I gestured for Mr. Irtaka to take a seat.

"No, I thought you might brief me on the projects you've been working on over coffee." "Okay!" I glanced at Khalid, who appeared confused and nervous.

"Shukran, Khalid, shyumkin Tarak." (Thank you, and you can leave.)

Khalid departed instantly.

"You're improving with the language," Irtaka remarked, admiration in his voice.

"Shukran, I'm merely trying to learn. It's rewarding to embrace a new language." As I settled into my chair, he presented me with a party invitation.

"I would be honored if you could join me for this gathering; it's crucial for the company's business," he said, sipping his coffee.

Peering at the invitation, I awaited further explanation. "Networking for the company!" He reiterated with a firm tone.

"Networking, understood," I replied, scrutinizing his expression.

"It's at Marina Garden, Burj Al Arab Jumeirah, Beach Road." He continued without hesitation.

"On the 4th of March, 2020."

4th March—my mind raced!

"And today is?" I tried opening my calendar.

"3rd March," he replied promptly.

Oh! How can he expect me to remain calm and collected under such pressure? "Mr. Irtaka, I'm afraid I've never attended such high-profile parties before; it may feel a bit awkward for me." I aimed to decline gracefully.

"I understand, but it's vital to socialize in Dubai for business," he asserted earnestly. His point was compelling.

Dubai thrives on social connections, and to thrive within such circles, one must engage with others. If they know you, they'll be inclined to work with you.

"It's been ages since I've mingled with people," I confessed.

"Well, that's evident," he gestured at my desk cluttered with files.

"Ok! I'll attend." Each time he presented a challenge, I felt ensnared. Ugh! "But first, I'd like you to review this."

I handed him a file labeled 'Children's Hope Foundation,' detailing an aging orphanage near the Trade Center.

"Can we please take on this project? This building is in dire need of renovation and basic amenities for the children!" I pleaded.

"I recognize the project may lack profitability, but the goodwill it would generate for our business—and the joy it would bring to the children—makes it worthwhile."

He regarded me thoughtfully. "What have you planned?"

Excitement bubbled within me as I prepared to share my visions and maps related to the orphanage. Suddenly, the atmosphere in the office grew quieter and darker. My eyes flicked to the watch.

Before I could speak, he suggested, "Let's discuss the rest over dinner." "Yes!" I welcomed the offer.

In less than half an hour, we found ourselves seated in a classy restaurant just two blocks from the office. My thoughts were consumed by the words Alia had shared, which felt so ironic compared to the real Mr. Irtaka. "So, how is your family?" He inquired, initiating a conversation.

"They're great! They might visit soon," I replied, my tone cheerful.

"That would be wonderful," he smiled.

"What are your thoughts on family?" He fixed his gaze on me, seeking an answer.

"To me, family is composed of those who truly know you and still choose to remain by your side. They trust you, no matter what, and serve as your unwavering support." He smiled quietly, absorbing my words.

Is he testing me? We continued our discourse, traversing topics from family traditions to outings.

"What subjects intrigue you?" He asked.

"History and Politics!"

"A compelling choice!" He remarked, visibly surprised.

"Is it because I'm a woman?" I raised an eyebrow playfully.

"No, I believe women with intellect possess a deeper understanding of such subjects than men." His sincerity resonated.

"Yes, like my mother; she was a professor of history and language," I shared.

"And your father?"

"My father was a Major General in the Indian Army, known for his blunt political views," I spoke proudly.

"Did you inherit their views or merely their interests?" He asked, amusement lighting his eyes.

"We held differing opinions, but our debates granted me a deeper understanding of the system."

"What subjects ignite your passion?" I asked, curiosity piqued.

"Literature has always been my refuge; it offers an escape from reality!"

"Why desire to escape from the beauty surrounding you?" I inquired, eager to learn more about him.

"To draw closer to that beauty," he replied, locking his gaze with mine. He continued, and I listened intently, forming a rosy image of him in my mind. "Literature provides insight into different eras and fosters a profound understanding of humanity—its struggles, coping mechanisms, and evolving intellect."

He radiated warmth and kindness, holding a rare belief in humanity's inherent goodness. Falling for him felt inevitable. "May I ask a personal question?" I ventured softly.

"Yes," he replied.

"Why is there no one in your life?"

A moment of silence enveloped us, and I realized I had overstepped. "I'm sorry; my curiosity got the better of me."

"It's fine; he hesitated not out of offense, but because he lacked an answer."

I gazed deeply into his eyes, pondering the unspoken reasons.

Our food arrived, pulling us back from that moment of introspection. We discussed the dishes, contemplating how they could be prepared differently.

A waiter approached. "Sir, it's closing time."

"What?" We exchanged astonished looks, realizing we were alone in the hall, a mixture of surprise, embarrassment, washing over us.

I offered my card for payment, but he replaced it with his own, adorned with an "IT" insignia. "What do the initials stand for?" I asked, curiosity piqued.

He shot me a serious glance, a silent warning that I had crossed a line.

Feeling slightly awkward, I fell silent. Did Mr. Irtaka harbor secrets, concealing them from the world while maintaining an air of mystery?

"What time is it? My phone is dead," I asked, seeking a distraction. He glanced at his watch before delivering the shocking news: "1:55 AM!"

"What!" I exclaimed, momentarily losing composure, before regaining my composure as we exited the restaurant.

An inexplicable feeling enveloped me; I found myself captivated by his presence. Every aspect of him—his words, accent, fragrance, humor, style, smile, and those eyes—held me entranced. In that darkness, I felt love creeping in.

Comfort enveloped me, was it wrong to feel this way? Or was I merely flirting with danger?

I felt a water droplet on my face, and in the depths of my imagination, I never would have fathomed it was a raindrop, so I dismissed it. Mere moments later, a torrential downpour began, catching us unawares. We dashed toward our car, parked across the street, laughter mingling with the rain as we sat beside each other, utterly drenched. I cannot speak for him, but my heart thundered in my chest. An unfamiliar flutter stirred within me, soon revealing itself as a perilous realization.

At that instant, I knew—I was falling for him!

As he navigated the road, clouds poured heavily as we arrived at my home, soaked yet exhilarated. He turned to me, and we exchanged smiles, joy blossoming like a flower in spring, for this felt like the purest connection I could ever envision with another. As he prepared to leave me on my doorstep, an urge surged within me, fueled by my newfound emotions. Before he could take another step, I broke the silence, whispering, "Would you like to come in for some coffee?" Did I speak that aloud? Was it merely a thought? I stood there, heart racing, waiting for the truth to unfold.

He turned back, a smile gracing his lips, and replied, "Sure."

Oh, how delightful! I had indeed invited him for coffee. A moment of shock washed over me, a whirlwind of emotions spiraling within—happiness, excitement, and a hint of sweet trepidation. In that moment, I realized we genuinely cherished each other's company.

I hurried to fetch dry towels and directed him to the bathroom. He looked around my home, adorned with personal touches. I had photographs and vibrant hues, especially in the bathroom, which boasted shades of soft pink.

He chuckled, "Pink!"

"A little!" I replied, a blush creeping to my cheeks.

"Just a touch!" he retorted, teasingly.

"I'll whip up some coffee," I said, retreating to escape the awkwardness of the pink.

I handed him the steaming mug while he perused the photographs on the wall, guessing the identities of those captured in time.

"You resemble your father," he remarked, tracing his jawline with his fingers. "Your mother seems much more disciplined," he added with a twinkle in his eye.

"She was!" I emphasized, "But Dad balanced it out for us." "Your sister appears to be the studious type."

I rolled my eyes. "Yeah! She always preferred doctor games over Barbie dolls." "And your brother? A football player, I presume?"

"Bull's eye, you've nailed it!"

His gaze met mine, and in that instant, time seemed to stand still. I felt the warmth of his eyes holding me captive, and we lingered in silence. Our connection felt extraordinary; we understood one another.

As we settled on the couch, the conversation flowed effortlessly, reminiscing about our cherished childhood memories. Recently, our talks had stretched longer, and losing track of time had become a delightful habit. Yet, deep down, I knew that "him" and "me" could never become "we." I understood that I needed to guard my heart, for I was dancing with fire, attempting to find balance in the flames.

He sat beside me, and Irtaka began to gently caress my face, tucking stray hair behind my ear. The coolness of his fingers sent delightful shivers down my spine. I nestled into his embrace, inhaling the scent of rain intermingled with his cologne. He pressed soft kisses on my forehead, claiming me as his own. I melted into his arms, feeling cherished, protected, loved. He murmured, "Yes, 'you' and 'I' can indeed become 'Us'!"

My phone rang, shattering the spell of my dreams. I glanced at him, peacefully sleeping on the sofa, and a smile crept onto my lips.

Stepping into the garden, I whispered, "Hello, di! How are you?" A primary question to veil my secrets.

"What's wrong? Why are you whispering?" She asked, concern in her tone. "I was just sleeping," I replied, attempting to cover up. "Tanisha, are you alright?" She probed suspiciously.

It's troubling when your sibling can sense your deceit.

"I dozed off while watching a movie," I explained. "Movie? Which one?" She inquired with curiosity.

"An Arabic film; I'm learning Arabic, so I thought I'd watch something in that language." I had covered my tracks well this time.

"Ah, your newfound passion for Arabic! Whatever keeps you busy and happy. I miss you!"

"Me too, di, and don't worry; I'm perfectly fine," I assured her, though I sensed the concern lingering in her voice.

"Okay! I must head to my morning shift, but I just wanted to hear your voice," she said affectionately.

"Alright, di! I'll call you later." I hung up, returning inside to find him sitting on the sofa. It was Azan time.

"I should go. I'll see you at the office," he said before leaving.

"Okay," I replied, smiling back.

As I stared at my phone, the fragments of my dreams swirled in my mind. I couldn't shake the thought that he would never love me, even if I had fallen for him. It felt like an illusion.

Rushing to the office, I collided with Alia.

"Are you alright?" She asked, balancing the files in her arms. I appeared composed but felt dizzy, sleep-deprived, and intoxicated by my emotions.

"Are you really okay?" Alia pressed again.

"Yeah, all good!" I said hastily, darting into my cabin to avoid further inquiries. When Mr. Irtaka entered, I was hidden behind a stack of files.

"Miss Tanisha!" His voice echoed through the room.

I stayed silent, gathering my thoughts before responding. He exuded an air of intimidation, and I couldn't let my feelings overwhelm me.

"Miss Tanisha!" He called once more.

I emerged from behind the files, our eyes locking, and my heart raced. "Thank you for last night. I had a wonderful time. It felt good to talk," I said shyly, handing him a file to sign, eager to divert my excitement.

He retrieved a pen from his pocket, and I noticed the initials "IT" engraved upon it.

The sight of "IT" on the pen sent a jolt through me. I realized he must have someone in his life. My heart sank, and I felt shaky, as if the ground beneath me had given way. I collected myself and shifted the conversation to business, discussing a few files, but I desperately needed a moment to regain my composure. I excused myself to the ladies' room, grappling with the realization that it was futile to fall for a man already entwined with another. His world felt unattainable, a distant star, and yet my heart ached with longing.

I cried quietly, reminding myself that I was merely human, susceptible to feelings that were universal. It took time to return to a state of calm.

Coming back into my cabin, I appeared composed, but my eyes betrayed me.

"Is everything alright, Miss Tanisha?" He inquired. "Yes, I'm fine," I replied with a smile. "Miss Tanisha, do you remember the party tonight?"

"Party! Oh, yes." it will serve as a distraction, I sighed

My expression shifted as I contemplated my wardrobe. Irtaka seemed preoccupied with the files, allowing me to sneak a glance at designer dress stores on my laptop. I felt low, but I knew I would recover in time.

"Oh! You're searching for dresses," he remarked, glancing at my screen. A blush crept in, leaving me speechless.

"Yeah! Formal attire would feel a bit out of place at a social gathering."

He smiled. "Allow me to show you a store after office. It's classy, and I believe it's just the right place for what you need."

I couldn't refuse his offer, as I had little choice.

At 6:30 pm, we departed the office, entering a lavish showroom named "The Saffron Saga by Tabeeya." I was awestruck by the collection displayed; the shimmering dresses, infused with a classy Arabic touch, left me spellbound. The challenge was choosing just one.

As I stepped inside, a radiant lady behind the counter greeted us with warmth. Her gentle demeanor and noticeable baby bump added to her charm. Dressed in a beige anarkali suit and brown hijab, she resembled a fairy. She smiled at me as though she recognized my spirit.

She welcomed Irtaka with a slight bow and extended her hand for me for a handshake. "Good evening, Miss..."

"Tanisha..."

"I'm Tabeeya. How may I assist you?"

"You have an incredible collection," I replied, shaking her hand firmly in return. She nodded, her smile coy as she excused Irtaka and led me on a tour. "How long until your baby arrives?" I inquired, glancing at her bump.

"Four more months to go," she beamed, placing a hand on her

She blushed as her hand lingered on her stomach.

"Aww, that's so sweet; all my love for you both," I said, and a shared smile illuminated our faces. Turning my gaze, I spotted Irtaka outside the store, engrossed in a call.

"So, what kind of dress are you envisioning?" She inquired.

"Something simple and subtle for a business gathering," I replied, my eyes wandering over the shimmering array of dresses.

"I'll send Shaanya to help you personally," as she duckwalked to the counter. I was spellbound by the collection, my heart fluttering over a few exquisite pieces.

"I think you adore the entire store," Irtaka whispered as he approached.

"Absolutely!" I replied, joy sparkling in my eyes.

"Go on and choose," he encouraged my excitement.

I glanced at him before turning back to the dresses; each one was a marvel, yet their prices were beyond my reach. Unable to resist, I drifted toward the glass showcase and immediately fell for a gown. The royal blue, double-layered linen dress, with its velvety texture and delicate silver zari work adorned with white pearls, was nothing short of magnificent.

"Please allow me to purchase this dress for you."

In that moment, Irtaka and I transcended beyond the dress, the price, the onlookers, and the whole store; it was about the bond between Irtaka and me. I held my breath, feeling the air thicken with unspoken words. His cologne, a familiar enchantment, made my heart race and we were lost.

We were startled when a salesgirl approached and Irtaka walked few steps away from me.

"It's a lovely choice," she said sweetly.

And I watched her in astonishment as she tore the price tag away, discarded it..

I opened my mouth to protest and looked at Irtaka.

He silenced me with a gentle gesture, signaling the bustling crowd around us. The wisest choice was to maintain a low profile.

"Ma'am, would you like to try this on, or shall we pack it?" The salesgirl asked.

"Please, she'll get ready for the party here; we're short on time," Irtaka instructed decisively.

"Very well, sir. Ma'am, please follow me; I'll guide you to the changing room." The salesgirl led the way, her expression a mix of surprise and delight. This time, I savored the moment, keeping my thoughts to myself.

Dressed in the gown, I let my hair cascade freely.

"Accessories with the dress are complimentary," Shaanya mentioned, showcasing them. They were utterly captivating.

The pearl-embellished deep neckline accentuated my collarbones, while the full net sleeves showcased my toned arms. I opted for minimal accessories: a delicate silver chain with a chic pendant and long dangling earrings that framed my face beautifully. A touch of mascara, a hint of blush to highlight my cheeks, and my favorite winged eyeliner completed my look. My black heels added an elegant touch to the ensemble.

As I stood there, the salesgirl entered, her smile radiant. "Tabdin jamilat jidaan," she exclaimed.

"Thank you" for I understood nothing more than that she was complimenting me.

Searching for Mr. Irtaka, I found myself filled with butterflies. I walked into the hall and found him in a navy tuxedo that perfectly complemented my dress. He was a vision; his tousled hair, piercing eyes, and muscular frame made my heart race with every passing second. My cheeks flushed as I felt his gaze upon me, a mix of shyness and exhilaration urging me to retreat rather than face him.

As I approached, our eyes locked, and my throat went dry.

"Masha Allah! You look beautiful," he said, his voice a soft caress.

"Thank you and you look fabulously smart yourself, Mr. Irtaka," I tried picking up a lighter tone in my voice. I approached the counter to express my gratitude to Tabeeya. She exuded warmth and radiated an aura of positivity. "Thank you ever so much for the exquisite dress; I shall surely return to your enchanting store."

"I would be thrilled to see you again, Tanisha," she replied with a beaming smile.

Turning my gaze towards Irtaka, I noticed him smiling at us from a distance. With a gentle gesture, he indicated that it was time to depart, prompting me to walk over to him.

As Irtaka and I stepped outside, an elderly lady cast her gaze upon us and remarked, "Ya lah min zawjayn jamilayn, aibqawa marikina."

Curious, I glanced at Mr. Irtaka for a translation, but he merely smiled back, guiding me onward.

Once we were on the Freeway, I seized the moment to inquire about the lady's words:

"What did she say?"

"The lady believed we were a couple; she blessed us with wishes for a long and healthy marriage."

"Why didn't you correct her?"

He fell silent with his smile lingering.

At loss for words, I chose silence as my companion for the evening, allowing me to focus on the art of socializing but how will I navigate my own feelings? My entire being felt awry, and my mind had descended into a haze. I felt utterly enchanted and warm by his presence.

CHAPTER 6

"Chaāp tilak sab chhīnī re mose nainā milāike

"Bāt agam keh dīnī re mose nainā milāike

As the car glided effortlessly over the flyover, the enchanting lyrics of "Chaap Tilak," my cherished Ghazal by Amir Khusro, rendered by the illustrious Abida Ji and Rahat Fateh Ji, filled the air.

The melody wrapped around me like a comforting embrace, soothing my frayed nerves. I realized that I had been overanalyzing everything and overthinking about Mr. Irtaka.

As we approached a grand entrance, the night erupted with dazzled lights. The vehicle slowed to a halt near the main hall, revealing a throng of media and celebrities, engaging in lively interviews, exchanging greetings, and showcasing their exquisite ensembles. This was my inaugural experience of such an affair, though I had watched countless Met Gala videos. The evening promised to be a whirlwind of excitement, far from the tranquil vision I had envisioned.

With a calmness that belied my apprehension, I stepped out of the car, reminding myself to maintain poise. Mr. Irtaka joined me, and I clutched his arm tightly; the crowd loomed large, and I could not afford to lose sight of the only familiar face in this sea of strangers.

We crossed into a vast expanse adorned with a musical fountain, where vibrant patterns danced in time with the Arabic melodies that floated through the air. The decor was a canvas of white, infused with a spectrum of colors that enchanted the senses.

"Amazing!" I breathed, captivated by the fountain's spectacle. "Hmm," he replied, gently squeezing my arm as a cue to follow him.

I was holding his arm, and in that moment, it felt as though he was leading me like a child, filled with wonder.

Upon entering the bustling hall, the crowd swirled around us, as I walked beside Mr. Irtaka. I felt the weight of curious gazes upon us, which intensified as the evening unfolded.

"Excuse me! Mr. Irtaka," I summoned my courage to speak.

"Yes?" He replied nonchalantly, seemingly unfazed by the stares.

"The stares," I managed to voice. "What do you wish for me to do about that?"

"Would you like a remedy?" He inquired, a playful smile gracing his lips.

"Yes, please! I'd be most grateful," I implored.

He leaned in closer, whispering with mirth, "Ignore them!" igniting a ripple of curiosity among onlookers.

"What!" I exclaimed, my eyes widening in surprise, continuing the charade.

This was the second instance since the dinner where he relished placing me in such a provocative position. A gentleman clad in a dapper black tuxedo approached us.

"Al-khair An-nur, Mr. Rehman." Irtaka beamed at him as they exchanged firm handshakes. I stood, observing their gestures intently.

"How have you been, and who is this lovely lady accompanying you?" He queried, his gaze shifting to me.

"I'm well, Mr. Rehman. Allow me to introduce Miss Tanisha Oberoi, our new General Manager," Irtaka announced, glancing at me with pride.

"Miss Tanisha, meet Mr. Rehman Qureshi, the Director of Mahira Associates, the leading consultancy firm in Dubai."

"As-Salam Alaykum, Sir," I greeted, extending my hand with a smile.

"Wa Alaykum as-Salam, Miss Oberoi. A pleasure to meet you," he replied warmly, turning to Irtaka. "I'm impressed; your company's shares have soared since your recent government collaboration proposal."

"Mr. Rehman, it was Miss Oberoi's brilliant mind that crafted the designs. The idea to collaborate with the government was entirely hers," Irtaka added, nudging me gently.

"He is too kind to give me credit, Mr. Rehman. Mr. Irtaka possesses many hidden talents," I replied, a smile gracing my lips.

"And hidden treasures as well!" Interjected a lady in a cream gown adorned with glimmering diamonds.

Her pointed remarks left me feeling uneasy, but I kept my composure.

"This is my wife, Abida," Mr. Rehman introduced her to me.

"So, you are the young lady we've heard so much about!" She exclaimed.

"Yes, Mrs. Abida, she is the new Manager, a treasure concealed from the world!" Irtaka remarked playfully.

"Not for long, Irtaka. You are the diamond; she will fade away," she said with a smirk. I stared at her, suppressing the urge to deliver a witty retort, but recognizing the importance of this gathering for the company.

"I doubt that, Mrs. Abida. Tanisha is my eternal gold," he declared, locking eyes with me. She fell silent, her expression shifting.

I savored the unspoken words; I cherished his response to Mrs. Abida, feeling my heart leap with joy. Irtaka held my hand, oblivious to the scrutinizing crowd.

Mrs. Abida's discontent was visible, and I sensed her irritation at his affection towards me. Mr. Rehman excused himself, guiding his wife away.

Irtaka introduced me to several other industrialists, yet my mind lingered on Mrs. Abida's barbed words. Irtaka translated Arabic phrases for me, inducing me into the new conversations.

"Good evening, beautiful," Irtaka greeted a gracefully attired lady in white. As she turned towards him, her radiant smile illuminated the room, despite her apparent age.

"Tanisha, this is Mrs. Humaira Hasan. She's the chief editor of 'La Moda Dubai,' one of the top magazines in

Dubai, and an old friend," he said, embracing her warmly.

Mrs. Hasan smiled, enveloping me in a hug. "You are a lovely soul!" She whispered in my ear. Observing Irtaka's hand intertwined with mine, her smile widened with genuine delight. "You look enchanting in that dress, Tanisha," she complimented.

As the evening wore on, I felt increasingly unsettled by the stares and disdainful glances from certain women in the crowd.

I glanced at Irtaka, who was engrossed in conversation with a group. Everything around me slowed to a crawl. "It's not you, dear!" Mrs. Hasan observed, sensing my discomfort. "You possess a sharp mind; rule the world."

"Thank you for your kind words, Mrs. Hasan," I replied, anxiously awaiting Irtaka's return.

The party offered a feast of diverse cuisines and appetizers. However, the sight of a camel beautifully adorned for biryani extinguished my appetite.

"Why do the ladies seem intent on murdering me with their glances?" I asked, trying to know the actual reason.

"It's not you! Dear, it's him," she gestured towards Irtaka. "Don't fret; they will grow accustomed to this."

"To what exactly? What do you mean by 'this'?" I pressed.

You'll know in time. and she excused herself.

"It's late; we should depart," Irtaka he said walking towards me.

The evening air was brisk as we exited the venue, and I shivered slightly from the chill and the underlying speculation. Noticing my discomfort, Irtaka promptly removed his coat and draped it over my shoulders. I wrapped myself in it as we settled into the car, allowing the highway to unfold before us, and I melted in my seat.

"Thank you! It was enjoyable despite the stares," I said, leaning back with a sigh. Irtaka glanced at me, "Thank you for what?"

"For the dress; it's simply gorgeous," I admitted, resting my hands on my lap.

He smiled, continuing to navigate the road. I could still catch a whiff of his masculine scent lingering on his coat, and the fabric felt comforting against my skin. But Mrs. Hasan's words 'with this' kept ringing in my head.

"It's complicated," he started speaking addressing question as if reading my mind. "People have never seen me with anyone, so they become intrigued by you."

"Why is that?"

"Perhaps because I'm always busy," he smirked.

His cryptic response left me unconvinced, and I sensed a shadow lurking beneath his surface. My own thoughts were tumultuous, and I felt my feelings for him spiraling out of control.

As he pulled into the driveway, a wave of melancholy washed over me at the thought of saying goodbye; I yearned for him to stay, but under what pretense?

"Allow me to escort you to the door," he offered, standing before my car door.

We walked along the porch, and I gazed at him with newfound affection, realizing how deeply I was falling for him.

I had encountered men before, yet none resembled him. He expected nothing from me; though he bore the title of 'the boss', he never wielded it arrogantly. His love for his homeland and pride in his faith shone brightly. He openly criticized those who stained God's name with bloodshed. Truly, he possessed a heart of gold, and I found myself enchanted, captivated by the essence of who he was.

Would he ever feel the same? I pondered. My heart ached with the knowledge that my feelings were but a solitary flame. It wasn't just my faith that set me apart; I was also an immigrant. I smiled at him, reconciling with the reality that what I cherished could slip through my fingers, never truly mine. "You are beautiful," he murmured softly.

I looked up, warmth blooming within me. "Thank you!"

"May I come in for coffee? I find myself hungry."

"Of course! Come in, I could use a bite too," I replied, as we stepped into the living room.

"Let me brew you some coffee and whip up something to eat while you change," he said, rolling up his sleeves and heading into the kitchen. I eyed him, smiling in agreement.

Was he truly willing to cook? Had he ever brewed coffee in his own home? In traditional Muslim families, men and boys typically did not partake in such tasks.

Yet, granting him this opportunity was a chance to discover his hidden talents. I dashed to my room, stealing a glance in the mirror. I wanted to savor one last look at my stunning dress before changing; a blush crept onto my cheeks as I admired how beautiful I felt today.

This evening was a dream. I was with Mr. Irtaka, who appeared equally charming. Now here he was, in my kitchen, crafting coffee for me. My heart raced to 150 beats per minute at the thought of him preparing coffee in my home; I feared it might leap from my chest. I hurriedly slipped out of the dress and into my nightwear.

As I emerged from my room, I found him in the kitchen, balancing a tray with two cups of coffee and buttery toast. He smiled at me as he made his way to the dining table.

I took a seat across from him, draping his coat over my chair, feeling his gaze linger on me as if he had something to say.

"Mrs. Abida wished to arrange a marriage for her daughter with me," he said, nibbling on his toast.

"And you used me to stir the pot," I retorted playfully.

He erupted in laughter at my words. "Not quite, Miss Tanisha! But I certainly wanted to escape that predicament."

As he spoke of various guests who could be potential customers or partners, I found my mind drifting solely to Irtaka. I gazed into his eyes, envisioning him closer, an overwhelming thirst stirring within me, longing for him, craving his warmth. My emotions surged uncontrollably.

Would he ever fall in love with me? Could he ever reciprocate what I felt? Would he embrace a Hindu girl in his heart?

Doubts flooded my mind, yet my feelings for him flourished. I recognized I was teetering towards an emotional abyss.

Now I understood why they say love is blind. Lovers tread a path they know may burn behind them, yet they walk it willingly. It's not merely the fog of confusion that leads them, but the daring leap of faith they embrace in love.

I was acutely aware that I had taken that leap of faith.

CHAPTER 7

After witnessing her today in "Al Farooq Omar Bin Kitab," I am convinced that Allah weaves our faith in wondrous ways. I stood, captivated, glancing at her, my heart rekindled in a manner reminiscent of my youth in India. I had vowed to keep her joyful, cherished, and safeguarded, to uplift her in every facet of life. Oblivious to the world around her, untroubled by the confines of any faith, she sat gracefully, offering her prayers to her Hindu deities.

"Bhai Jaan!" Rashid startled me from my reverie.

"Maulvi Saab is asking for you! Come," he pulled me innocently, turning to steal one last glance at her.

I stood there, entranced by her heartfelt devotion. Truly, Allah has preserved someone extraordinary for me.

"Abu is calling you, Bhai Jaan!" As he tugged at my arm, my Misbaha slipped from my fingers.

"Rashid! my Misbaha." I searched frantically but to no avail. It held deep significance for me; crafted by my mother to recite Allah's name daily, it had been kept close by my father for years. Only last Ramadan did he bestow it upon me, and I felt profoundly privileged.

"Bhai Jaan!" He called out again, and I turned, hoping he had found it.

Yet, his expression shattered my hopes, and I realized it was lost. A wave of despair washed over me. I inhaled deeply and looked once more, but alas, it was nowhere to be seen.

"Let us go greet Maulvi Saab. He must be waiting." My father often said that anything lost in the Mosque is not truly lost but embraced by Allah.

I returned to my spot, determined to search for my Misbaha one last time. I glanced at Tanisha, still seated, struggling with her hair.

Misbaha! She held my precious Misbaha I had lost, delicately wrapped in her hand. A smile blossomed within me, realizing Allah's blessings surrounded us.

As I walked out, my thoughts were consumed by the image of her beside me on the flight. I vividly recalled that night; her beautiful eyes were filled with tears, mascara running from her sorrow, chapped lips and red, watery gaze revealing her anguish. Though I longed to comfort her, it was painful to witness her grief. Even her fleeting smiles were a struggle. Her emerald eyes, the blush on her cheeks, and the perfect outline of her lips made her undeniably captivating. She slept next to me, as if the world had ceased to exist. I pondered what the fates might hold for us. I wished to hold her hand, to assure her that I would stand by her today and for all time. I should have revealed my identity, but perhaps I was selfish—like a star I admired her sitting so close.

The next day, my eagerness to see her was palpable; I yearned to witness her reaction upon discovering my truth. She entered the boardroom, fear visible on her face. I delighted in her fidgeting fingers, the way she adjusted her hair, and her struggle to smile. My heart swelled as I saw the color drain from her face upon recognizing me. She shifted uncomfortably in her seat.

She seemed acutely aware of the the IT logo everywhere in the office, even on the laptop screen while working on the presentation. "Someday," I sighed internally, "I'll reveal to her what 'IT' signifies."

In the car, she sat beside me, her gaze fixed upon me, reminiscent of our flight. I wished desperately to decipher her thoughts. Suddenly, she shouted my name, her grip on my shoulder igniting a fire within me, my heart racing wildly.

Since her arrival in Dubai, my feelings for her have been hard to control. Her presence is magnetic. How will I ever confess the depth of my love for her?

Days and weeks slipped by as I struggled to find the courage to speak with her. Her dedication to her work only deepened my admiration. I watched her closely, arriving early to work and playfully placing pens between her soft lips as she immersed herself in files. She still fought to maintain her composure.

Witnessing her in the rain was a sight to behold; it felt as if droplets awakened the petals of a flower, bringing forth vibrant colors.

When she invited me for coffee at her home, I was overjoyed. We shared tales of childhood memories, family, and books.

With each conversation, I felt myself inching closer to her. Her warmth radiated in every gesture, even as she remained unaware of my affections.

Her free spirit can never be contained; it is destined to soar. Her eyes, the most mesmerizing beauty in my life, hold me captive, and I am losing myself within them.

Catching her browsing for clothes was amusing; she shyly retreated, speechless.

At Tabeeya's store, I couldn't divert my gaze. She embodied the pinnacle of creation! Gracefully moving, her eyes sparkled while her lips curled in shyness. The royal blue dress made her look enchanting, like a princess from a fairy tale, rendering even the stars and moon pale in comparison.

I was at a loss for words to compliment her. Her allure captivated me, leaving me breathless.

She grasped my hand. Was she anxious in the crowd? I held her hand tightly, overwhelmed by the privilege of this connection, vowing never to release it and to bring her boundless joy.

She loved the musical water fountain, her eyes sparkling with excitement. Though her worried expression amused me, she handled the stares with remarkable poise.

I strolled beside my star beneath the moonlight, feeling complete and wishing for nothing more.

As she gazed at me, searching my soul through my eyes, I longed to convey my feelings—to promise her my respect, my protection, and my unwavering support, to allow her to discover her desires and wait until she chose us. Yet, I understood that now was not the moment.

On the couch, she slumbered, capturing my heart with every breath. How could I ever articulate her significance to me? Deeper and deeper, I am falling in love with her. I was neither a prince nor a Romeo; I felt like a lover captivated by Stella, the furthest star. I knew little of love but understood enough. There is no turning back. She lay before me, so near yet so far.

—⋏⋏—

Birds chirped in the garden, and sunlight streamed through the window panes, waking me up. I shifted on the couch and spotted Irtaka on the floor, his head resting against the sofa, lost in peaceful sleep.

I felt an intimacy with him, though a distance still lingered.

I wished time would freeze at this moment, allowing me to live alongside him for eternity. Rather than getting up, I snuggled deeper into the couch, stealing glances at his beautiful morning visage before finally tiptoeing to make coffee.

Standing there, coffee in hand, I grappled with the decision of whether to wake him.

"Irtaka," I whispered softly, addressing him informally for the first time, attempting to wake him up while fighting the urge to let him rest.

He looked up, apologies tumbling from his lips. "I'm sorry; I didn't realize I had fallen asleep." He ruffled his hair in a charmingly disheveled manner.

"It's okay, Irtaka. It was late, and it was better for you to stay. Would you like some coffee?" I offered warmly.

"No, I'll take my leave." He rubbed his eyes gently. "Alright, I'll enjoy both cups then," I teased, hoping to lighten the mood.

He stood, expressing gratitude. "Thank you. Yesterday was a memorable evening." He locked eyes with me, not waiting for a reply before departing.

I remained there, coffee cup in hand, watching him leave, my desire to kiss him intensifying. I felt parched, yet it was more than thirst. As I sipped my coffee, my mind spiraled into wild fantasies. I traced the delicate edge of the cup, imagining his lips against mine. Closing my eyes, the rich, creamy latte filled my mouth, igniting a longing within me. My breath quickened, and I shifted on the couch, consumed by the thought of kissing him, unable to escape the fantasy. Clutching the cup closer, the soft warmth against my lips made me yearn for him even more, and I closed my eyes, savoring the moment.

Reality crashed upon me, and I blushed, grappling with the forbidden thoughts.

CHAPTER 8

The office hummed with newfound energy for the first time in weeks!

A gathering of mostly middle-aged men and women, accompanied by a handful of spirited youngsters, awaited in the lounge area. Some sipped tea, while others were absorbed in the glow of their phones.

"Alia, what is happening? Who are these people?" I inquired, making my way toward my cabin. "Ma'am, they are teachers," she replied, her voice sweet as honey.

"Teachers?" I echoed, raising an eyebrow in curiosity.

"Indeed! They've come with the children from the orphanage. We are considering an orphanage project," she explained, her smile illuminating the room.

I paused, studying Alia for a moment. I was not taken aback; deep down, I had known he would take the orphanage project to heart.

"Mr. Irtaka invited the orphanage children to share their thoughts on the designs, their color and pattern preferences for the building and their rooms." Her tone conveyed a sense of awe at his unexpected kindness.

I made my way to Irtaka's cabin, spotting children emerging in a line, their hands brimming with chocolates. I watched as Irtaka filled their pockets with treats, their faces alight with joy.

"Good morning, Mr. Irtaka," I greeted, my voice radiating happiness at the scene. "Here," he said, handing me the orphanage file, "From the action plan to wall colors, all have been decided and approved by these little cuties. You were right; the children miss so much in their childhood." He met my gaze and smiled warmly.

"You did all this?" I asked, perusing the file.

"No! Not entirely! The kids lent a hand too." He unwrapped a chocolate and popped it into his mouth. I was momentarily speechless, for Mr. Irtaka was exhibiting a side of himself I had never seen.

He waved at the children and leaned closer to whisper, "Thank you! Miss Tanisha." I raised an eyebrow.

A stillness enveloped us, filled with trust, gratitude, and mutual respect. "So, where shall we dine today?" He asked as we entered his cabin. My cheeks flushed, and I glanced around, hoping no one had overheard.

"You missed the morning coffee!" I retorted, my tone had a playful sarcasm.

"Perfect, I'll drop by at 6:00 for coffee," he murmured, a charming smirk dancing on his lips.

"Sure!" My heartbeat faltered for a brief moment, and my mind drifted toward previously unspoken desires, now vividly painted against a sunset backdrop. In a flurry of emotions, I merely gave a thumbs-up.

In my cabin, I pondered the tangled web of my feelings. Was this healthy? I couldn't voice the question aloud, not even to myself. Yet, there was no denying the shift between us; from our first flight to last night, each encounter had woven our smiles tighter. Were we friends, or was there something deeper?

My inner self rolled its eyes at me. Friend-Zone Irtaka? Really?

He likely didn't share these sentiments. He was simply delightful, always placing loyalty to his people above all. They would never endorse this relationship, and how could I forget IT? Someone special must occupy his heart. My internal debate cast a shadow over my thoughts, and I chastised myself for the over-analysis.

"Miss Tanisha! Is everything alright?" Alia's voice pulled me back to reality as she entered my cabin, files in hand.

My expression betrayed my unease.

"Yes, just feeling a bit under the weather. I think I'll leave early today," I replied softly. "Do you need anything?" She asked, her gaze searching my face.

"No! Thank you, Alia," I said, refocusing on my laptop screen.

I found myself home early—perhaps for the first time since arriving in Dubai. The battles between my heart and mind grew heavy; my brain grilled my heart, making me feel guilty for my emotions. I scrutinized the differences between Irtaka and me, and the impossibility of harmonizing our worlds.

As I rearranged the flower vase and curtains, my heartbeat quickened, uncertainty creeping in. Was I giving him the wrong signals? Was I fostering intimacy? I felt the blood drain from my face, and suddenly, I froze as the doorbell rang.

"Irtaka," I murmured under my breath, moving slowly toward the door to open it. "Ma'am, Mr. Irtaka has sent a car for you," the driver announced, his tone informative.

Confused, I glanced at my phone for any messages from him.

"I'm sending a car to pick you up. I will see you soon," the message read.

I looked at the driver and nodded, "Five minutes."

I quickly changed into a strappy white floral dress and let my hair fall loose, hoping to shed the weight of those unnecessary thoughts.

My mind shifted from guilt to curiosity about Irtaka. What must he be thinking?

The car slowed near the bay, turning toward the dock area, finally halting beside a boat adorned with twinkling lights and minimal decor. I spied Irtaka standing on the cruise, clad in a simple white polo shirt and casual shorts. I had never seen him in such relaxed attire, and I admired how effortlessly he carried himself.

As the sun dipped low, painting the sky in hues of pink and orange, I joined Irtaka on the cruise ship's dock. We exchanged occasional glances and smiles, a silent connection blossoming between us.

"You look beautiful," he whispered, inching closer.

"And you complement the evening," I replied shyly.

As we sailed through the Arab Sea, a waiter served us Turkish coffee in delicate cups, the rich aroma wafting through the air.

With each sip, the bold flavor and fragrant essence washed away my stress, soothing my spirit. The small ceramic cup, adorned with charming floral designs, felt smooth and delicate in my hands.

"Are we friends?" I asked, gazing into my coffee while stealing glances at him.

He looked at me with an amused smile, eyebrows raised in surprise at my question.

What was I thinking? Embarrassment flooded me, and I turned my gaze to the waves, awaiting his response.

"Yes, of course we are," he replied cheerfully.

His words resonated within me, igniting a wave of excitement. My eyes sparkled, filled with emotions of satisfaction and security. I longed to embrace the moment without overthinking.

"Yes! We are friends," he declared louder, sensing my hesitation. I turned to face him fully.

He extended his hand for a handshake, gripping mine firmly. "Miss Tanisha, I propose that you be my friend from this day until the last breath of my life." His eyes sparkled with childlike enthusiasm.

"That was so cheesy!" I laughed, squeezing his hand. "Yes, from this day until my last breath, I will stand by your side, your partner in crime and friend forever," I replied, my smile radiant.

As the cruise came to a halt, he looked at me and asked, "Are you ready?" "Ready for what?" I exclaimed, a look of shock on my face.

"You'll see," he said, rising from his seat, removing his shoes and placing them beside the chair before striding to the ship's edge.

I watched, anticipation coursing through me, as he leaped into the water.

Fear gripped me as I rushed to the ship's rim, my heart racing as he disappeared for a moment. Then, he surfaced, waving at me joyfully.

To my astonishment, he was surrounded by dolphins. I stood there, utterly captivated.

Irtaka swam toward them, and I realized these dolphins were his companions. They chirped and danced around him, leaping joyfully in a playful embrace.

He gestured me to join him in the water!

Though excitement bubbled within me, fear held me back. This was a rare chance to be with dolphins, and before I could overthink, I slipped off my heels and jumped in.

The water was brisk; I struggled against the waves until suddenly, I felt something brush against my feet! Panic surged through me as I thrashed in the water.

Irtaka grasped my hand, and warmth enveloped me. He held me close, his embrace reassuring.

"They won't harm you; they just want to play," he assured me. Again, I felt a smooth touch against my feet.

"Ooh! Oh my God!" I gasped in delight.

The dolphins circled us, and I could reach out and touch them. One dolphin kissed me, sending shivers down my spine. Irtaka held me tightly, in his embrace. I clutched one dolphin, and it propelled us deep into the water before leaping high above. The first jump was a challenge, but with each attempt, I found my rhythm. It was the experience of a lifetime, and I savored every moment, diving repeatedly, completely lost in joy.

As darkness fell, we rested on the open dock, exhilarated yet exhausted.

"Thank you! That was incredible. I have never experienced anything so beautiful," I said, my eyes shimmering with gratitude.

"That's what friends do!" He replied, his sweet voice accompanied by a warm smile. "Yes! That is what friends do!" I echoed in my mind, the sarcasm lingering.

"I did not have many friends in my childhood, so I spent most of my time here," he began, his voice imbued with fervor.

"We claimed this stretch of beach, and to draw in visitors, I proposed the idea of having pet dolphins in the open sea, transforming this locale into a captivating attraction. Since then, the dolphins have flourished, and the surrounding businesses have thrived. I make it a point to return here to be with the dolphins; I miss them dearly." A joyful smile lit up his face, it was the first time he was opening up deeply.

"My mother died in childbirth! And I was the reason." His tone shifted, heavy with emotion.

"You cannot blame yourself for that," I offered gently, hoping to lighten his burden.

"She was a woman of remarkable strength and intellect; her beauty captivated all, and she was loved by everyone. Joy surrounded her; she epitomized the perfect daughter and daughter-in-law, yet the Almighty did not bestow upon me the gift of her presence." I witnessed his heartache, his voice trembling as vulnerability enveloped him.

We sat in silence, gazing at the waves as they danced and retreated; while the soothing rustle of the sea embraced our quietude.

"Jamila," he said, a smile gracing his lips.

I glanced at him, seeking clarity, mindful of my faltering Arabic. "Beautiful!" He clarified, casting his gaze toward me.

Ah! The sea, indeed, is a vision of beauty.

CHAPTER 9

The office hummed with an unusual stillness; I had arrived early, buoyed by a smile and a lightness in my step.

Then, I saw Irtaka enter. Our eyes met, and I raised my hand in a distant greeting. Yet, as I approached, an unsettling energy enveloped him. His clothes were crumpled and stained with blood, and a somber shadow loomed over his features, his eyes swollen as if mourning a deep sorrow.

With dread knotting in my stomach, I whispered, "What happened?"

He turned toward the office balcony, his gaze fixed on the ground, lost in a storm of thoughts. He raked his fingers through his hair repeatedly, struggling against an invisible weight.

I stepped closer, my voice firm yet gentle, "What happened, Irtaka?"

He met my gaze, his eyes heavy with unspoken words.

"What happened, Irtaka? Please, just tell me," I urged, taking his hands in mine. Leaning against the wall, he drew strength from my presence and murmured, "Dad! He met with an accident!" His voice quivered, and tears threatened to spill from his eyes, which he valiantly tried to conceal.

"How and when did it happen?" I held my racing heart.

"He was driving to the office and suffered a cardiac arrest. He's in the ICU," he replied, the weight of the news settling like a stone.

"Irtaka, he will be fine," I reassured him, gently ushering him into my cabin. As he sank into the chair, I poured a glass of water and placed it in his trembling hands.

"You must be with your father. He needs you. With you by his side, he'll recover swiftly. I promise to take care of everything here," I said, soothingly rubbing the back of his palms.

He met my gaze and nodded, then turned toward the door, pausing as if to speak but ultimately falling silent as he walked away.

Moments later, Alia entered my cabin, her spirit shattered. "Are you okay?" I inquired, enveloping her in a tight embrace.

She broke down, her sobs echoing through the room. I offered silent comfort, patting her back until her cries subsided. After a moment, I handed her a glass of water, and she settled into the chair.

"I was 15 when Abu and Irtaka Bhai Jaan adopted me," she began, her voice trembling with emotion. "Abu was always so kind; he shared every meal with me, feeding me by hand. I felt cherished and safe. He homeschooled me, igniting my passion for learning. Within months, I was fluent in English and Urdu. His love enveloped me; he brought me chocolates and pets from the shelter. His devotion to animals and gardening filled my heart with joy. Abu invested his time and effort in me, helping me graduate from Dubai University—it was a dream come true for someone like me. I owe my life to Abu." Tears streamed down her cheeks.

I absorbed each word, holding her hand as I learned about Irtaka's father and the bond that connected them all. I had always thought Alia was merely Irtaka's cousin, but the revelation deepened my respect and affection for their family.

A gentle knock interrupted us; Mrs. Dalia entered and embraced Alia, whispering prayers and kissing her forehead. "How are you, my child?" She murmured.

I stood by, watching them converse in Arabic, sensing that Alia was sharing details of the accident and the hospital's latest updates.

"Alia, please go to the hospital and be with Mr. Irtaka," I urged. Mrs. Dalia nodded in agreement, encouraging her to go.

I dragged myself in the office, my heart yearning to be by Irtaka's side. The thought of visiting the hospital weighed heavily on me; my past experiences there haunted my mind. I was paralyzed by the memories of my parents' fragile forms being wheeled away, the blood staining the floor—a chilling wave coursed through me.

I sat in the dim office, enveloped by fear, staring into the shadows.

The next day, I entered my office, thinking about Irtaka every step of the way. I saw Irtaka standing in my cabin. Our eyes met as I came, and we looked at each other, forgetting the world around us; we stood there without moving. He was tired and looked like a mess, a beautiful mess indeed! I so wanted to comfort him in any manner I could. He had not slept and looked drained out of his energy. Before I could say anything, I felt people around looking at us.

"Good morning, Irtaka. How is your father now?" I asked to release the awkwardness of the moment.

I heard a knock on the door. Alia stood there, unable to hide her worries.

"Come in, Alia!" I said in a soft tone.

She entered the room and handed me a file, looking worriedly at Irtaka, she said.

"Doctor has said that the next 48 hours are crucial for Abu." Turning her gaze towards me, she said: "Irtaka Bhai Jaan, come directly to the office as there is a meeting in half an hour." Alia was great at sensing people, so she said this on Irtaka's behalf.

"Meeting about?" I asked in a shocked state of mind.

Irtaka spoke in a low tone, "Meeting with the police officials." I looked at Alia and then at Irtaka for an explanation.

"Doctor believes it was not the cardiac arrest that made him lose control of the car. Police investigated thoroughly, believing the car has been tampered with."

"Okay," I looked directly at her as there was more to it.

"The car he was driving was not his; it was the vehicle from the office sent for Abu. His car had been broken for a few days, so he asked the office to make it available. You had gone home early that evening, so your car was sent for Abu's use." Alia finished speaking and kept a hand on my shoulder.

My heart sank as I spoke, summarizing her words. "You mean that someone was trying to harm me, and unfortunately, your father got hurt."

He nodded in approval.

I felt as if I had dodged a bullet and sat there shocked.

"The Police wish to ask you a few questions for your safety. I will inform you when they are here," Alia said, giving us some privacy.

"Irtaka, but I don't know anyone here," addressing him informally for the first time out loud. "Why would someone try to kill me?"

Instantly, my thoughts went to Kaashvi and Vinayak. I didn't want them to worry, so I started fidgeting with the Misbaha.

"I will ask Alia to stay with you for a few days until the police figure out who is behind it." He said

"Hmm," and I said nothing else.

He stood and looked at me, "Don't worry, I am there for you." I smiled weakly and looked out of the window.

Irtaka called several times and walked up and down the office balcony. I sat there, reasoning why anyone would ever want to harm me.

As the police personal came, Irtaka sat across the table while the Police interrogated me.

"How many people do you know in Dubai?" An official asked. I knew a handful, none of which would hurt me. "Do you have a boyfriend?" One of them asked.

I felt awkward about the question but knew it was part of their investigation.

"No, I don't have a boyfriend," I answered sternly.

"Any ex-boyfriend?" He continued,

"No ex-boyfriend!"

"Any family grudges?"

"No!"

"Any arguments in the past year?"

"No!"

"Any history of stalkers?"

"No, Sir!"

"When did you come to Dubai?"

"A few months back."

I knew I was not helpful in any manner. But I had no enemies. "We heard your parents died in a car crash."

I looked at them with painful eyes but did not understand where they were taking it.

"Enough, Officer. I guess it's all she can help you with," Irtaka said harshly to stop them from investigating more. The officer said nothing and stood up.

"We will keep you posted with our further investigation," and left Irtaka's Cabin!

But the remark on my parents' car crash opened the wounds; it left me wondering for the

first time, what if it was not an accident? Maybe their car was tempered similarly. Perhaps it was a murder? I was shocked.

"Water?" Irtaka held a glass of water in front of me as I looked at him dumbstruck.

"Relax," he pulled a chair in front of me and took my hand.

"Irtaka, the Police just questioned my parent's accident! What if they have a theory? What if they were killed." I said, all terrified thinking of the possibility.

"Shhh! Relax, drink water. Come, I'll drive you home." He said while standing up and walking towards the door.

I was quiet and lost on my way back.

We entered my apartment, and he locked the door behind me. I could not let the memories of my parents on their last days go.

I sat on the couch and thought about my dad, the last days he was with me; I did not leave him even for a second. I was by his side in the ICU; he did not open his eyes even for a second while I just sat there waiting for the moment he would. I did not want to lose my dad as I had already lost my mom.

Irtaka sat beside me on the couch, trying to calm me. I stood up, "I'll make coffee," I said and excused myself.

I kept the coffee mug on the side table and sat beside him.

"Do you miss them ?" He asked falling back in the on the couch.

"Yes!" I replied, my voice cracking.

Prophet Mohamad imparted, "Obeying and loving one's parents is paramount, for they selflessly sacrifice for their children."

It was a heart-wrenching sight to witness his pain. I longed to alleviate his suffering.

"Let's eat something!" I urged, gently pulling him from the couch.

Together, we somehow managed to cook. I wondered how our bond had deepened. Just a day prior, we were reveling in shared joys, and now we found solace in our mutual love for our parents.

As I prepared noodles and french fries, he perched on the kitchen counter.

"You know, once I fell ill, and my father devoted a week to nursing me back to health, canceling all his meetings. Today, I felt utterly helpless; I couldn't do anything for him." His words carried weight, but the true depth of his feelings shone through his eyes.

I gazed at him in silence and shared the meal, after the last bite, he asked, "Would you mind if I sleep over?"

"Of course not! I'll fetch you some fresh clothes and blankets," I replied, clearing the table while offering him a faint smile.

I left him in the drawing room and opened my wardrobe. My fingers brushed against an oversized t-shirt of my father, and the floodgates opened; tears streamed down my cheeks as I sobbed on the floor. I yearned to let go of my strength. I collapsed, weeping heartily when I felt a presence behind me. Irtaka settled beside me, enveloping me in his arms, soothing my back and wiping away my tears. Throughout the evening, I had forgotten he was my boss or that we differed in faith; we were united in our shared sorrow. Our love for our parents was a binding force, and as we cherished their teachings, I felt the weight of my longing and his fear of loss.

He held me close, and I didn't want him to release me from his embrace, I found solace; his strength mended my broken spirit, and warmth surged within me. This was our first hug, and in that moment of emotional vulnerability, he became the missing piece in my heart. Resting my head against his chest, I closed my eyes.

"They must be watching over you and would be immensely proud. All you must do is find happiness," he murmured. I nodded through gentle sobs, eyes closed, as he tucked a strand of hair behind my ear, leaning back against the wall.

Sunlight graced my face, coaxing me from my sleep. I blinked my puffy eyes, realizing we had slept on the floor, entwined in each other's arms.

As I shifted, Irtaka held me tightly, a hint of fear flickering across his sleeping face. The sudden ring of his phone startled him, the screen read "Hospital."

"Hello!" He answered, scared.

A woman's voice carried over the line, calming his features. "Hmm! I'll be there in half an hour," he replied, disconnecting the call.

"Dad is safe and out of danger. I'll be there when he wakes."

"He'll be fine, don't worry," I whispered, offering a reassuring smile.

In that moment, he realized he still held me. Our gazes locked, conveying a multitude of unspoken sentiments, yet we lacked the courage to voice them.

"I'm sorry for yesterday," he said, rising to his feet.

"You should go to the hospital. I'll see you later; don't worry about the office," I suggested, redirecting the conversation.

He glanced back at me, concern etched on his face. "Will you be okay?"

"Yeah, I'll be fine, just go!"

As he departed, I reflected on our differences. Were they truly significant? Irtaka and I shared so much: our outlook on life, our responses to challenges, our passions, and our reverence for our parents. What separated us? Religion.

Different faiths teaching us similar values. Throughout the evening, we had held hands, shared tears, and even slept side by side. Such bonds may defy our religious doctrines, but in humanity, this connection is simply being present for one another, sharing in the weight of sorrow.

My phone chimed with a message from Irtaka, "Take care."

CHAPTER -10

I stepped into the office, wearied from my visit to the orphanage. As I entered my cabin, a white note caught my eye, resting on my table.

"Coffee!" It proclaimed, and I turned to see Irtaka standing there, handsome, radiating a magnetic charm, a composed visage adorned with that delightful smile.

"Dad is discharged and will be alright in a few days. He's regaining his strength," he announced, his voice brimming with joy.

"Shukar!" I murmured, attempting to settle into my chair, but Irtaka swiftly lifted my bag and motioned for me to rise.

"I am treating you for a coffee and then dinner. Also, I have something to show you," he said, urging me to step out of the cabin.

I was acutely aware of the whispers that would arise in the office regarding our growing closeness, yet I brushed aside the thought. Their opinions mattered little; deep down, I knew he didn't love me.

As we sat in our beloved coffee shop's open area, fatigue enveloped me, leaving me drained and overheated. Irtaka, seated beside me, inquired, "Are you alright?"

With a faint smile, I nodded.

"You don't seem okay. Is something troubling you? What is it?" He asked.

"Nothing," I replied, struggling to suppress my tears and the low energy pulling me down. "I'll have coffee and be fine."

"Alright," he acquiesced, though doubt lingered in his eyes.

Gradually, Irtaka's voice faded, the world around me dimming. I jolted my head, but dizziness washed over me like a tide. Focusing on Irtaka's face became an arduous task, and soon, the edges of my consciousness blurred into nothingness.

As I closed my eyes for a fleeting moment, in that instant, I harbored no grievances against life, no battles to wage, no anxieties to mask—just an overwhelming sense of peace. A shiver coursed through my body, and Irtaka picked up on it.

"Are you feeling cold?" He asked, concerned.

"A bit," I murmured softly.

"But it's 42 degrees today!" He exclaimed, worry clouding his eyes. He reached out, brushing his hand against my forehead. "You're burning with fever, Tanisha!"

In that moment, the truth of my pain became clear, and I understood the source of my disorientation. Heat surged through me, mingling with a sudden chill.

"I'm fine. I just need coffee," I managed to utter.

"No, we're heading straight to the hospital," he insisted, worry lacing his tone. "No, please, not the hospital! It makes me feel worse."

He extended his hand with a nod, and I, too weary to argue, followed him. He took me home and checked my temperature.

"You have 103 degrees, Tanisha! This is far too high."

I sat there, my senses dulled, as if I had consumed an entire bottle of rum; I felt nauseated. As I stumbled toward the bathroom, my legs gave way, and I collapsed into his arms.

His cool hands brushed against my fevered cheeks, and he cradled me with tenderness and comforted me. I longed to believe in this moment that he loved me, yet the reality that he didn't love me weighed heavily on my heart. Tears streamed down my face, not out of desire for his adoration but from the knowledge that he is not in love and will never love me. Despite the chasm between us, I found myself falling deeper for him, craving his presence by my side.

"Shhh."

"It's alright. I'm here, and you will be fine. I believe it's just a fever and food poisoning. Let's get you to bed and find some medication."

I felt too weak to move, so he held me tighter. All I wanted was to cry, wishing my fever and heartache could be soothed with my tears. I wept as I took the pill, and he sat by my side, holding my hand. After that, my senses faded into darkness.

I felt a pinch. Was he trying to wake me up? I lacked the energy to open my eyes. A cold sensation coursed through my veins. Am I dreaming, or is this the chill from the fever? Why is my bed moving? Is it my bed or me? My pillow is stiff. What's happening, Irtaka?

A female voice broke through my dreams.

"She is waking up!"

I blinked and sought the source of the voice. Alia!

What is she doing here? My body felt stiff, and I noticed IV drips attached to my hand. As clarity began to return, I spotted Alia, a doctor in a white coat across the room, and finally, there was Irtaka! He looked disheveled and worried.

I met his gaze, and relief washed over him.

"What happened?" I inquired of Alia, who hovered near my bed.

"You had a high fever and were unconscious for 12 hours," she explained without pause.

"Just a long sleep, perhaps!" I attempted humor, though it felt forced.

"The doctors were worried; they kept you in intensive care," she continued, gently rubbing my forehead.

Looking around, I saw his anxious faces, and it dawned on me why Irtaka appeared so worn.

After Alia departed, leaving us alone, Irtaka approached my bedside, and I couldn't resist his gaze. He took a seat beside me as I finally focused on the room's inviting decor, which felt worlds apart from typical hospital settings. The large flat screen and expansive window framed a breathtaking city view. The soothing white and blue tones enveloped me in comfort.

"How are you feeling?" He asked, genuine concern lacing his voice. "Better," I replied softly.

"I was scared," he confessed, a look of dread on his face.

"Have you eaten anything?" I inquired, noticing his fatigue.

"I'm fine," he assured me, even though his face and body said otherwise.

Questions swirled within me, but the words stuck in my throat. Why was he so worried? What fear gripped him? After all, we were merely friends. But all I could say loud was,

"Thank you."

Breaking the silence, I asked, "What happened?" My mind needed clarity on how I ended up in this hospital bed.

His expression shifted, and I noticed the tension in his jaw.

"You had a high fever. After taking your medicine, you fell unconscious. I thought you were merely asleep. I sat there, waiting for you to wake or shift, but you didn't budge. Hours passed before I called the doctor. She suggested taking you to the hospital, and we brought you here."

My phone rang, and I spotted it in Irtaka's hand.

"Your phone," he said, offering it to me.

"Hello! How are you now? Feeling better? Irtaka informed me about your fever and unconsciousness. I was about to board a flight, but he advised me against it. I've spoken with your doctors, and they assure me you'll be fine, but you must focus on your nutrition," Kaashvi rattled off without pause.

I glanced at Irtaka, who smiled as I responded to her questions with murmurs.

Did he speak to her? How did he introduce himself? What must she think? How would I explain it to her, the endless discussions about society and religion? My mind swirled with unease.

"I'm fine. I'll call you later. Bye. Yes, I'll eat well and take care." I ended the call and shot Irtaka an irritated glance.

"What did you tell her?"

"I told her I was your friend, that you were hospitalized and unable to talk due to your fever. I asked her not to worry, assuring her we were all here for you," he continued in a calm, reassuring tone.

I realized how much he cared; he'd stayed by my side while I lay unconscious troubled me. He had been there, watching over me as a friend. I clung to the lie, holding onto his presence regardless of what we both denied to acknowledge.

The doctor had prescribed a strict diet, and blood samples were taken. Irtaka chose a room that accommodated guests, and I knew he wouldn't leave my side.

As evening fell and the lights illuminated the city, I felt a sense of comfort under Irtaka's watchful eye.

"Irtaka," I whispered, just in case he hadn't heard. "Hmm!" He replied, focused on the blood reports.

Now or never, Tanisha! I said, bucking myself up "Can I ask you something?"

"Of course," he said, his Arabic accent softening his words.

"Do you have a girlfriend?" I inquired, my voice barely above a whisper. The room's silence amplified my question, and his eyebrow shot up in surprise.

And in that moment, I cursed myself thinking, if he had one, Tanisha, would he be sitting here in the hospital with you, his tired eyes reddened from sleepless nights spent for a friend.

"Forgive me for asking. The answer is not needed; it's perfectly fine. We can simply watch TV and muse over politics, food, or any topic that tickles your fancy."

"Shhh!" He interjected, engrossed in the file in his grasp.

I sealed my lips, inhaled deeply, and held my breath. Was Mr. Irtaka truly shushing me? Yes, indeed! He silenced me with a finger pressed to his lips, and I complied. Resuming my meal, I sighed as I slurped the bland soup, the sight of the boiled vegetables extinguishing my appetite. I reluctantly chewed on a cooked carrot.

"A star is easy to follow, a delight to behold, yet remains ever out of reach," he mused unexpectedly, breaking the silence. He stood gazing out the window, perhaps thinking of her.

"But you must pursue that star, allowing it to feel your affection and care," I replied, eager to engage in his contemplation.

He shot me that peculiar look once more.

Ah, so he wasn't speaking in reference to her.

"You know, as a child, I believed starfish floated among the heavens," I blurted out, instantly regretting it. Seriously! Was that the best you could conjure, Tanisha? You're in deep trouble! I admonished myself.

"I think sleep would serve you well; your medication is taking effect," he said with a playful smirk.

What does he mean by that? Do I resemble a cartoon or a tipsy soul when my medicine kicks in? I decided it was best to sleep rather than dwell on it any further and regret later. I closed my eyes. "Good night," he said, dimming the light and settling into his own bed.

The nurse stirred me awake for my medication, and as I gazed at the stars outside, I realized it was still night. "What time is it?" I inquired.

"It's 4 AM," she replied sweetly.

I tried to keep my voice hushed, fearing I might disturb Irtaka, but to my surprise, he was already awake, engaged in prayer.

As the nurse departed, I watched him in that serene moment, his calm demeanor illuminating the room. I felt a wave of comfort wash over me, not from the medicine but from his presence. I could only imagine how my parents would have cherished his unwavering support, grateful for the kindness he showed.

Lost in thought, he approached my bedside and placed his hands gently on my face, as if imparting a blessing just received. I met his gaze with a smile, aware that our religions diverged, yet recognizing the universal value of morning prayers. I lay there with open eyes, silently thanking the unknown force that safeguarded us.

As sunlight streamed into the room, I opened my eyes to find Irtaka beside me, watching intently. How long had he been observing me?

Why was he gazing at me when I look like a complete wreck?

"You look beautiful!" He said, as if reading my mind.

Did he just compliment me? Tanisha, this isn't the first time he is praising you, but it felt different this time—intense, profound, and so much more.

I locked my green eyes onto his blue ones. "Thank ..."

"Good morning!" We both jolted from our sweet moment, turning our attention toward the doorway. Alia!

She appeared contrite for her sudden entrance at such an awkward moment. I attempted to sit up, and Irtaka assisted me, propping me up on his shoulder and arranging the pillows.

What is he doing? He is boldly announcing to the world that something is brewing between us. I shot him a worried glance, concerned about Alia and the doctors nearby. Yet, he simply smiled back, nonchalantly dismissing my anxieties.

Am I overthinking this? Perhaps, but he wouldn't jeopardize his reputation over "ME." Aren't these people truly imagining wild scenarios about Irtaka and me? And if so, why does he remain so unfazed? If he appears calm, why does it trouble me so? His entire reputation is at stake: the expectations of his community, his family, and above all, his father. What if they discovered the extent of his care for me?

He is simply kind to me, but is he perhaps falling for me?

Tanisha! How dare you entertain such thoughts? You know he would never fall for you; it's merely the hospital's circumstances and your illness.

"I'll be away for four hours due to a series of meetings. Until then, Alia will keep you company," he informed me, turning to Alia. "Make sure she takes her medication and doesn't overexert herself." He looked endearing, playing the role of the concerned caretaker.

I stifled a smile, finding it charming how Mr. Irtaka was so protective and insistent about "NO WORK."

As he departed, a flurry of doctors and nurses flooded into the room, their busy energy indicative of emergencies, and I became the sought-after patient they were eager to treat.

I lay there, observing the diverse faces around me. The doctor appeared to be from China, while the nurse hailed from South India.

Once the flurry subsided, Alia and I found ourselves alone. She settled into a chair a distance away, adhering to her instructions.

"Alia, please come sit beside me," I implored.

"Miss Tanisha, I've been instructed not to disturb you," she replied, sounding like a soldier following orders.

"Alia, I'm alright and feeling better; I just need someone to talk to. Please, drop the 'Miss Tanisha' formality. You know I despise it."

Finally, she moved closer and smiled. To break the silence and steer away from Irtaka, I asked, "So, how is everyone in your family?" I knew it was an odd topic for us since we rarely discussed family matters. "And how's everyone at the office?"

"I know you have feelings for him," Alia said suddenly.

I stared at her in shock. "It's not like that, Alia," I stammered, desperately trying to mask the depth of my emotions for him. I had never said those words to myself out loud, yet denying my feelings felt impossible.

"He's changed so much since you arrived. He's happier, more focused, and full of life. I've never seen him so joyful."

I listened, processing her words.

"Miss Tanisha, you should rest. Your illness frightened Bhai Jaan. I've never seen him so worried about anyone since Abu." She continued, "He's quite different around you," she remarked, a smile gracing her lips. I turned to her, seeking clarification on what she meant by him being different with me.

"I've worked alongside him for over six years. He was always quiet, focused, and buried in work. He barely spoke to anyone. When he returned from India a few months ago, one day, Bhai Jaan came into the office smiling. We were all stunned but celebrated his joy. Since then, he's smiled more often, yet he never interacted with us until you came along. You are the first person he's opened up to, accompanying him to meetings with ease. It's evident he cares for you deeply, and seeing him so vulnerable, worried, and caring, I believe he loves you." Her eyes sparkled, and her smile radiated pure happiness.

I knew I had feelings for him but was terrified of acknowledging them. Is he grappling with the same fears? That question loomed in my mind, unanswered. I remained silent, knowing I had nothing to say to Alia, yet denying her thoughts felt essential.

"No, Alia, he's not in love with me. He's simply a kind person. We share common interests, but he is not in love with me." I offered a smile, knowing we could neither predict the future nor truly understand it, but I chose to deny her beliefs.

We shifted our conversation to market trends, discussing the famous camel milk chocolates and premium-quality dates, our dialogue drifting to the sweltering weather in Dubai and the local fashion. Alia recounted her explorations in various markets, particularly 'Bur Dubai,' renowned for its textile shops boasting vibrant fabrics and exceptional quality, along with 'Wafi Mall,' where she found vintage artworks, and 'Mina Bazaar,' famed for exquisite gold jewelry designs. Our conversation blossomed into wanderlust, laughter echoing as I recognized how much I had missed.

As the sun dipped below the horizon, I suggested Alia head home. She understood my need for solitude. I smiled and thanked her.

The room settled into silence, yet Alia's words reverberated in my mind. I pushed them away, knowing he would never fall for me. Even if he did, there was no future for us. Alone and frightened, I sobbed quietly, feeling my grip on reality slip away. Suddenly, I felt Irtaka's arms around me, pulling me close waking me up from my sleep and calling my name, assuring me I was safe and not alone, I was just having a bad dream.

"Shhh! It was merely a bad dream," he whispered, enveloping me in a protective embrace. "I am here!" His words wrapped around me like a spell, binding us together. In that moment, I knew my heart was succumbing to love's gentle pull; I had accepted that he was indeed the one for me.

We remained still, suspended in time, perhaps grappling with the emotions we hadn't addressed. The world outside faded away, leaving us cocooned in warmth and safety. Irtaka eventually pulled back, bringing me water, tenderly wiping my tears away as he settled beside me.

I was undeniably in love with him, yet this love brought with it a bittersweet ache, for the fear of losing him loomed over me like a shadow. And with that, a deeper fear brewed within; a gnawing uncertainty clouded my thoughts.

What lay behind his eyes? What secrets danced in the corners of his mind? What if he was as emotionally entangled as Alia had suggested? Who was the elusive

'IT'? The love of his life? And where did I fit into this tangled web of affection?

The heart of the matter was that I remained blissfully unaware of his true feelings. One moment, he drew me close, and I felt like his alone; the next, reminders of 'IT' crept in, a haunting presence that stood between us, casting a long shadow over our connection.

"Rest," he said softly, retreating to his own bed.

In the stillness of the room, silence reigned, but inside we were locked in a battle against the tumult of our emotions. Our gazes met, each searching for the other's soul. Deep down, I longed to shout my love from the rooftops, yet I was forced to keep it hidden from the very heart I adored!

"Sleep," I urged him, knowing he was weary and worn.

"Are you okay?" He inquired once more.

"Yes, I'm fine. You're the one who needs rest."

With whispered goodnights, we slept with our thoughts.

As dawn broke, I woke up to the gentle caress of sunlight streaming through the window. The nurse arrived with my medications, and I gestured for her to tread lightly, for he was still asleep.

Seated on my bed, I gazed at his captivating face, watching as a faint smile played upon his lips, gradually giving way to a slight clenching of his jaw that accentuated his striking features. My fingers danced over my phone, capturing the moment in a video. I zoomed in on his serene expression; he appeared unburdened, a world away from his usual self. I couldn't help but wonder about the secret love that occupied his heart—what enchantment had captivated him so completely?

He shifted gently, hugging the pillow with an innocence that seemed foreign to the man I knew. When awake, he carried the weight of the world, yet here, he was a child, cocooned in dreams.

The mischievous side of me re-emerged as I was recording him peaceful sleep. Suddenly, my phone rang, and as I scrambled to silence it, the sound startled him awake, his body jolting toward me.

"Are you okay?" He asked, concern etched across his face.

Guilt washed over me, mixed with frustration at the interruption, but his reaction stunned me. He was openly expressing his feelings, showing genuine care, yet I still struggled to accept this as love.

"Are you okay?" He asked again, his voice all worried.

"Yeah, I'm fine."

He raked a hand through his hair, and the nurse checked my temperature, declaring it normal.

"Does that mean I can go home?" I glanced at the nurse, hope lighting my eyes. "The doctor will decide that, dear," she said with a composed demeanor. Irtaka settled beside me once more.

"How do you feel now?"

"I feel better," I replied with a smile, "just eager to return home."

"Alright, if your fever doesn't return by noon, I'll arrange for your discharge." "Thank you," I said, feeling a wave of relief wash over me.

But I could not take my mind off his reaction, is there something that he is hiding from me.

CHAPTER -11

"Love Jihad and Conversions" by Rashmi Oberoi. Rashmi Oberoi boldly rebukes the ' Right-Wing' and the left wing for their spurious claims. The headlines in 'The Hindu' blared this news in striking letters.

I stepped into the vacant classroom where Professor Rashmi was immersed in her papers. "Professor, do you have a moment?" I tapped gently on the glass door.

"Irtaka! Yes, do come in; how are you? Where have you been?" She replied, removing her glasses with a warm smile.

"Good afternoon, Professor. I'm doing well; I spent a week in Bangalore," I said, settling into a chair before her desk.

"You bear such a resemblance to your mother," she remarked, gazing at me fondly. "Your eyes and smile evoke memories of her every time I see you. She was my dearest friend."

"I wish I could have known her as you did; it warms my heart to discover the echoes of her spirit in your writings."

"Indeed, she was very fierce, honest, unafraid to be the voice of the voiceless, and her heart yearned to travel the world, much like you wish to do."

"The article offers a unique glimpse through the lens of a Hindu," I remarked.

"Yes, it is penned not merely by a Hindu but by a fellow human who decries the shadows of terror, unjustly accusing young Muslim boys and young women and complicating their lives, diminishing their place in society. This, in turn, leads to a cycle of unemployment, suppression, exclusion, and dwindling opportunities," she replied, gently tucking away a few papers into the cupboard.

I sat there, a silent observer, absorbing her words and actions as she articulated her deep-seated concerns.

"I know Inter-religious love marriages are difficult. They challenge various norms and customs while questioning the faith of religion. I believe these kinds of intimacies often provoke conservative forces with their anxieties and fears, and a conservative group in India with anxiety and fear creates hell for women, children, and vulnerable people while breaking the boundaries of human cruelties. There are hate campaigns on topics like homosexual love or inter-caste and inter-religious romance while portraying them as one of the biggest threats to cohesive community identities and boundaries, which in turn serves the purpose of political parties, fulfilling their agendas and personal interests."

"The latest example added to the list is the false constructs by the politicians commonly termed as 'Love Jihad' or 'Romeo Jihad'," she said, now getting breathless. I wish I could change the world's mentality a little." She looked at me, sighed and smiled slightly.

"How may I assist you? And she brushed off her thoughts, you seem burdened; share your thoughts with me," she said, her gaze piercing through my unease.

"Professor, there's something," I replied, searching for the right words within the confines of my mind.

She locked her gaze onto mine, "Alright! I'm all ears! Please, proceed."

"During my time in Bangalore, I encountered a few friends working as software engineers; they developed a database to monitor the campaigning activities of political parties across Kerala, Karnataka, Maharashtra, and Delhi. A project born from their own initiative..."

"Organizations under the pseudo name and groups with no faces are actively holding meetings, distributing pamphlets, and filing false court cases declaring that Islamists have devised plans for compulsive and deceitful religious conversions," I said and waited for her reaction.

"This was what I was concerned about." She said while thinking deeply about something and yet kept listening

I continued, "They even profess that Muslim youth are receiving funds from abroad for purchasing designer clothes, vehicles, mobile phones and expensive gifts to woo Hindu women and lure them away; the ramifications of such a campaign is to foster hate for its anti-women overtones and to create panic. The protests against such a vicious attack have been witnessed lately in many states. Professor, this hate will haunt us for centuries if not stopped. If we don't take action, this hate will pave the path for riots, racism and communal distress. 'Love Jihad' is one of the agendas of the campaigning in many states," I said in one breath.

She blinked at me and said nothing for a few minutes. "How sure are you, Irtaka?" She asked sternly.

"Professor! The data is drawn from local campaigns, local newspapers, pamphlets distributed locally, underground meetings, anonymous Facebook posts, Instagram feeds, etc.

Rumors have it that the campaign will operate in a public domain to monopolize the minds of the greater public."

She sat there numb without uttering a single word.

"Irtaka, now listen to me. You will do as I say. You will Fly back to Dubai tonight, and give me the numbers of your friends."

"But Professor! We must unveil those orchestrating these violent, deceptive protests; it is imperative to enlighten the masses about how these factions are ensnaring them." I rebelled, casting a defiant glance at her regarding the notion of returning to Dubai.

"Who will you educate? Irtaka. Do you even know who they are? They are anonymous, like shadows, and have no face."

"Professor, I am not scared. I will stay here to help you," I said with aggregation.

"Irtaka, you will be scared when you see the riots, people being butchered in the streets, women being raped, and hatred growing to an extent where humanity ceases to die. Yes! I do have a liberal voice in our democratic country, but Irtaka, there are consequences every time I write something with my conscience and intellect. My family is threatened; my students are harassed. I am bullied on the streets." She said, trying to explain to me the pain.

"So, you mean we do nothing about it. It is just talks and articles and write-ups and debates." I said, fuming in anger.

"Irtaka there is no 'we' here. You will do as I say, and I want you safe on a plane to Dubai, tonight!" She said in a concerned, low tone.

"No, Professor! I need to stay here and be the voice!"

"Not a word, Irtaka! You are going back home. Karan and I promised Raad that we would take care of you. You are our responsibility."

I knew I had lost the argument with her, but I could not go. "But Professor, I love her!"

She sat in the chair and said nothing for a few minutes.

"I know, Irtaka and I understand you will keep her happy, but my daughter has the right to choose her life and her life partner. I cannot take that away from her."

"I understand," I said in a low tone.

"But, Irtaka, you must promise me that you will keep her safe no matter what happens." She said, looking straight into my eyes.

"I promise I'll keep her safe with my life, professor."

She came close, hugged me, and kissed my forehead, "Tell Raad we miss him." Few hours later, I was on a flight to Dubai.

That fateful moment marked the final glimpse I had of her. The news of the car accident struck me like a bolt; I was ensnared in shock for days, burdened with guilt for returning to Dubai. Deep down, I understood that this was no mere coincidence; it was a sinister facade for murder, orchestrated by a malevolent group. To this day, I bear the weight of self-reproach; I should have never departed, fully aware that shadows lurked, willing to do anything to silence her and sow chaos. Since that dark hour, my mission has been to shield Tanisha from danger and conceal the harsh truths that linger in the shadows.

My love for Tanisha gives me strength. Although she is unaware of the world outside, I am amazed by how she wishes to change it with respect, just like her mother.

I have come a long way from feeling guilty about loving a non-believer, but who decides who is the believer and who is not? The unrest created was an equal attempt by Hindus and Muslims in the Delhi riots.

Allah! Let the believers be the humans who believe in humanity, not the ones who kill in the name of God and ruthlessly destroy the gift of life that you have given us.

CHAPTER 12

Irtaka was driving me home while I nestled in the car, enveloped in the mellifluous notes of Abida Praveen Ji's song.

"Nit kher manga money mein teri dua na koi hor manga,

Tere pairan ch akeer hove meri dua na koi mangdi."

Elated by my discharge, yet feeling the weight of potent medicines that left me weary, I savored each lyric, resonating deeply within my soul. As we approached, I saw Alia at the door, with a radiant smile.

"Can we sit in the garden? I'm not quite ready to step inside," I implored with hopeful eyes towards Irtaka.

"You need to rest, Tanisha," Irtaka murmured gently.

"Please, Irtaka. I crave some fresh air." I pleaded, summoning my most enchanting puppy eyes, thinking I could sway him.

"Bhaijaan, basking in the sun will uplift her spirit."

I smiled and took a step towards the porch which felt like a distant ease, I took hesitant steps, leaning against the car for support. I was not ready to believe what Alia had said, but I chose to believe that it could be a mere 'infatuation' or 'Tau Waqti' for him, and he has a soft heart for me.

While I sat amidst the blooming garden, basking in the sun's warm embrace, Irtaka suddenly inquired, "Would you both care to join me for dinner tonight? I have made some delightful reservations."

"Bhai Jaan, I regret to say I cannot join, as I must remain with Abu at home," Alia replied, graciously excusing herself.

"Absolutely yes," I responded and smiled inwardly.

As I stepped out in the evening wearing a blush pink maxi dress with ruffled sleeves and high collared neckline, I could feel the breeze against my skin, and I shivered, which made Irtaka wrap me up in a white shawl, and in a concerned tone, he said.

"We can cancel the reservations."

"No! I want to go Irtaka," and I fast-forwarded a few steps and seated myself in the car.

As we stepped into the restaurant, we were greeted by vibrant Bollywood decor, showcasing actors and actresses adorned in dazzling attire, alongside whimsical 3D paintings of autos and trains. The dining area boasted a cabaret-style stage, reminiscent of an open mic or karaoke, dedicated solely to the enchanting melodies of Bollywood. The music wafting through the air transported us back to the late 1960s. I was utterly captivated by the atmosphere, for my heart danced to the rhythms of classic Indian songs and cherished Bollywood films. We found our seats beside a glass window, where a grand camera aimed its lens in our direction, ready to capture the magic of the moment.

"Itna na to mujh se Yun Pyar Badha main hun Badal Awara" came up, and I looked around excitedly as if someone had purposely played the song. I smiled at Irtaka, wondering if he understood any of it. I sang along slowly and rested my back in the chair.

The waiter handed us the menu, but I knew what to order.

"Let me order for you, please!" Irtaka requested and took away the menu from my hand.

"As you say," I said and sat there listening very carefully.

"Chicken tikka, for starters. Butter chicken accompanied by butter naan and vinegar onions for the main course and hot Gulab Jamuns in dessert," In one breath, he said it all as if he had memorized it.

The waiter smiled and noted, "Enjoy your evening, Sir."

I looked at Irtaka for an explanation. He smiled, and his smile turned into unbridled laughter.

"Irtaka!" I looked at him, laughing, and said nothing, confused and almost cracking up. I waited for him to sober up from his laughter.

"Indian restaurant, my favorite songs, and my favorite food. What is going on?

"Today, after Kaashvi spoke with the doctor, she told me how to revive you back to health in the shortest amount of time; that's when she sent me your favorite menu and a playlist of Hindi songs!" He said with a shy smile.

"Yeah! The playlist was not some random playlist; it was my playlist," I smiled, thinking about his efforts to make me comfortable.

"Thank you, Irtaka."

"That's the least I can do!" He said while listening to the next song's lyrics and humming the tune.

"Chura liya hai tumne jo dil ko, nazar nahi churana sanam."

I was surprised by his gestures. I sang the songs in my mind and hummed, but my eyes were glued to him, and he reciprocated the stare with his heart-warming smile. I wondered

What are we doing? I needed to know why we were fighting it back? but I feared confronting him, so there was a "loud silence" between us.

"Mom was an excellent singer," I said, breaking the silence. "She had memorized several songs for Dad." Irtaka sat there listening as I kept singing and explaining the lyrics.

Mom's favourite song was "Aap ki nazron ne samjha pyar ke kabil hume, dil ki ey dhakan tehar ja mil gya sahil hume, apki ki nazron ne samjhaa." I hummed the song and caught glimpses of him listening to me.

As our food arrived! I indulged in the first bite of my chicken with vinegar onion. I looked at Irtaka, who sipped his lentil soup very diligently.

"Please help yourself, " I said, offering him the chicken plate. "Thank you, but I am vegan!"

I looked at Irtaka in shock and then at my plate. "But you are a Muslim, and you live in Dubai!"

He looked at me, amused by my notion, and smiled.

"Yes, I am a Muslim, and yes, I do live in Dubai, but I believe food is a matter of choice for an individual."

Embarrassed by my judgement, I smiled and slowly took another bite of my chicken tikka. I kept quiet for the rest of my dinner and feasted on Gulab Jamun. The waiter cleared our table, and I sat back, listening to the songs in the background.

Irtaka kept a box in front of me. It was a red velvet ring holder.

I looked at him in astonishment; my hands trembled as I touched the velvet box. I anticipated this to be his confession of love.

What is it? I asked

"Open up and see for yourself." He said in a calm tone.

"Irtaka" I searched for words to make a sentence but could not even think of an alphabet.

"Open! You won't be able to say no," he said, moving the box towards me.

What! Does he know about my feelings? Did Alia say something? Maybe! she smirked at me in the afternoon and did not accompany me because she knew he would propose. I was cold and couldn't figure out what I would tell Kaashvi and Vinayak. They have no idea about my feelings for Irtaka, who is a Muslim and my boss. My brain drifted into its slow-motion zone. I could feel and sense everything so minutely and couldn't stop overthinking.

"Please open!" He looked at me with excitement to open the box.

I took the box in my hand, closed my eyes and flipped the box open.

As I opened my eyes, my heart stopped briefly, and I looked at Irtaka. I glanced at the box and saw shiny white-coated medicine. I wanted to cry, shout, and, like a child, lay on the floor and throw tantrums. I was pranked!

"Medicines!" Really? I looked at him with an annoyed face. Medicines in a ring box! I slow-clapped for his prank because I had been pranked badly.

Irtaka was laughing so hard that he lost his voice.

Seeing him laugh so hard, I smiled but gave in to the laughter in a few seconds because I could not ignore Irtaka's laughter. The song "Chahe koi mujhe jungli kahe" came up, and we both gave in again to our laughter.

"Damn! That was cruel, Irtaka," I exclaimed.

"I always wanted to prank someone other than my brother but never got a chance." He said with a burst of uncontrollable laughter.

"How long did you plan this prank?" I asked, still annoyed with him.

"I was with Alia when she showed me a piece of jewelry she had bought for dad. She packed it in a fancy-looking box, which made this box useless, and that's when it struck me."

I sat there thinking about how big of a fool I was and how I could even imagine him proposing to me.

We left the restaurant feeling light and still laughing about the prank. I was a bit disheartened, but somehow, I felt better.

"You will catch a cold," he said, putting my shawl on my shoulder. He came closer, and we stood close enough, staring into each other's eyes, that I wanted to tell him how much I loved him.

"Tanisha!" He said, moving away and not looking at me. I want to talk to you about something."

"I am listening!" I said, setting my shawl.

"Not here! Let's go to the beach." I could see the joy building up in those beady eyes.

"Beach at this hour?" I asked questioningly

"The beach at this hour is quiet and peaceful. Let's go to the beach! Please," he said with hope and opened the car door for me, gesturing me to take a seat.

"Sure, the night is beautiful." While I sat beside him, I noticed his expression change; he seemed lost in his thoughts.

We did not talk much while on our way to the beach; the night had grown darker, and I could hear the rhythmic sound of the waves until we reached the parking lot.

We took off our footwear and headed towards the part of the beach owned by Irtaka. While I was observing the beautiful waves and the moon, he said, "Tanisha, you know, in our religion, a man has the liberty to marry anyone he desires."

"But it is limited by many conditions!" I completed his sentence.

He looked at me and said nothing, as he knew I was right; we continued walking when I decided to break the silence. "So, you are thinking of marriage! Nice," I said in a sarcastic tone.

"Tanisha!" He paused, "Come sit here," and pulled me on the bench nearby."

We sat on the bench, watching the sea waves in the distance. Scrunching my toes, I could feel the soft golden sand underneath. The far-stretched sea and the limitless sky seemed to meet somewhere that appeared impossible to reach. It reminded me of our impossibly beautiful love story, which seemed far from reality. I was wandering in my thoughts when Irtaka interrupted.

"Tanisha," I need to tell you something."

"Please go ahead and say," I turned my body towards him.

"Recently, I have been fighting so much inside me with the faith I follow, expectations of my loved ones, promises I have made, and most importantly, my love for someone." He said while looking at me and trying hard to get words out of his mouth.

There was a pause; I sat there quietly, watching him struggle with words. Irtaka brushed his hands in his hair and said, "My love," looking at me.

Wait a minute! Damn, did he just address me as his love? I can't believe this.

Taking my hand in his and kneeling before me, he continued, "Tanisha, I feel for you; you are the one. I love you!"

Wait, what? Can someone please rewind the moment? Did he tell me he loves me? Me! Tanisha Oberoi, I was stunned. I looked at him with no facial expressions. I had nothing to say; it was as if I had reached my destination and realized that I loved the journey.

I was numb, speechless, and had a brain block all at once. I closed my eyes tightly, blinking it twice to get rid of the effect. I wanted to move, say something, and try to express myself; instead, I sat there stiff, finding it difficult even to utter a single word. I inhaled deeply and breathed out slowly through my mouth twice.

Tanisha! Your medicines are working! I told myself. "These are some severe pills," and I scoffed.

"I love you!" He said again, a bit louder, slowly moving closer to me. He looked deeply into my eyes and held my hand tighter.

"Since when, Irtaka?" I spurted out my question!

"Since the day I saw you Tanisha, I love you so much," he repeated with utmost sincerity and love.

So, does that mean I am not dreaming? A cold chill spread throughout my body. I looked at him with surprise, still thinking about how to react.

I had no other plans than to express my feelings out loud. I never thought I would ever be able to communicate. Now what? Come on, Tanisha. It is not rocket science.

"What do you mean?" Shit! Did I ask what you mean? Shit! Screw you, Tanisha. You are a dumbass, sick ass, total ass. "I am sorry for asking you that. I feel blurred out." I apologized.

"I even love you when your medicines work on you." He said and planted a soft kiss on my hands.

A giggle escaped my mouth. "So, will you repeat everything when I am not on my medicine?" I said dumbly.

"Yes, I will repeat my love for you every day until my last breath, Tanisha. I will also wait until you feel the same, or even if you don't, I will respect your decision."

He sat there watching me smile; his gaze felt like sunshine on a cold winter morning. He was my sunshine; it was a new morning for us.

"Irtaka, I have so many things to say. I prepared myself days and nights to express my feelings for you, but now, when I have the opportunity, I have no words; I am blank."

"Okay! Just tell me, do you feel the same as I do?" He said, patiently waiting for my reply. I looked into his eyes and whispered, "Ana' ahbik, Mr Irtaka' Ana' ahbik." He pulled me closer in his arms and cupped my face with his warm hands.

"Really?"

I moved my head in the up-down direction because words were far too much, and I had no voice for them anymore.

He hugged me tightly, holding me in his arms; I embraced him back. I still could not believe this was real; I always thought it was my dream and wanted to live in my thoughts forever. We walked towards the car hand-in-hand, smiling at each other the entire way, stealing our moments.

As he drove, I sat ogling at him and smiling like a child. I was bursting with questions and needed clarification on whether to ask him.

"Ask me!" He said while smiling at me.

I looked at him in astonishment; what! Is he reading my mind, or am I thinking loudly?

"You make that face when you want to ask something, but you fight inside your mind to ask or not; that confusion shows on your face."

And Irtaka turned the mirror in my direction; I saw the lousy face I made: lips frowning, eyebrow raised in the center, and the end of the nose tilted to the right side.

"Chi! I look so horrible!" And how many times has he seen me like this? It ought to be my pig face.

"So, how many faces do I make?" I asked out of curiosity. "I have seen you in your,

'Reading face': You have your glasses on while you play with your nose tip, moving it 360 degrees when you read. Also, you rarely blink while reading, this shows the amount of concentration you put in your work, and I'm so damn impressed by that.

'Serious face': You don't give any expression but roll your eyes, breathe slowly and blink your eyelashes when you do not seem to like some ideas.

'I am such a happy face': You have the broadest smile, your nose tends to grow fast as it's stretched to the sides, your eyebrows are raised high, and you swing your ponytail in the air while having a bouncy walk.

'Angry face': You tend to have lines on your forehead, which make you look older; clenched teeth make your jawline clear from the right side of your face.

'Writing face': When you write, you focus so much on your handwriting that you either chew your lips or take your tongue out as if you are balancing yourself on a rope."

"Irtaka! How long have you been noticing me?" I asked in a state of shock.

He stopped the car and looked at me. "Since the day I saw you!" He said and hugged me softly.

He drew nearer and pressed his lips gently to my forehead. His touch crackled through my very being, awakening a deep yearning within me; I surrendered to the depths of his ardor. As I wove my fingers through his hair, he drew me closer, and I longed for every precious inch of him. Each caress intensified his presence, culminating in our first kiss—his lips brushed against mine like the softest feather, a sensation unlike any other against my skin. My desire grew insatiable, and I kissed him fervently, my hands gliding up and down his back.

We stood at the threshold of our sanctuary; he lingered at the entrance, gazing at me, while I remained within, a mere whisper of air separating us. With a gentle embrace, he wrapped his arms around my waist, pulling me tightly to him. In that moment, our eyes locked, and our noses touched, eliciting shared smiles that made the world around us fade away. His grip tightened as he tenderly caressed my back, and I felt my breath quicken. The sweet mingling of our breaths enveloped me; my hands ventured into his hair, his touch ignited my skin, sending shivers cascading down my spine, awakening every sensation within me.

I arched in his arms, and only then did he touched me again, but this time, he did not hold back his kiss but took a step forward; my lips were his possession, which he lovingly explored.

He closed the door while we stood there feeling each other. I had never experienced this joy in my life. I could not ask for more because of the touch of his hands on my body, his lips on my lips, and his love on my soul.

I was so joyful that I could not stop making love sounds; the more I let the sound escape, the more kisses intensified. His lips on my neckline made me gasp. We could not hold ourselves standing, and we fell on the couch.

"Ouch!" My head bumped on the table, and that made us pause. "I'm sorry, really sorry I did not see that," we both said. Our smiles turned into shyness; I tried to hide my face in his chest. and kept my head on his chest, listening to his heartbeats while he played with my fingers in his hand.

"When I saw you at the board meeting, you were so scared that you kept rolling your ring. I wanted to hold your hands and tell you how much you meant to me."

I listened to him with my eyes closed while he continued to tell me what he had been feeling all this time. I shifted my head in his lap, and he traced my face with his fingers. He patted softly on my cheek and pushed away my hair locks behind my ear, which soothed me, and I drifted off to sleep beside him.

CHAPTER 13

"Good morning, beautiful," he whispered in my ear, planting a soft kiss on my cheek. A smile blossomed on my lips as I rubbed the remnants of sleep from my eyes.

"Good morning; how did we come to bed?" I inquired softly.

"When you were asleep, still smiling, I cuddled you and brought you here," he replied, enveloping me in his warmth once more.

Today felt different; I was cocooned in his embrace, glued to his chest, savoring his tender affection. He had borne his soul, uttering the three magical words that possess the power to transform lives and worlds.

"My coffee cup," he declared, kissing my forehead gently.

"Coffee cup!" I exclaimed, gazing up at Irtaka in astonishment. "Since when did you become so cheesy, Mr. Irtaka?"

"Since the day I fell in love with you, Miss Tanisha."

"That is a big, fat lie, Mr. Irtaka."

"And how so?" He asked, pulling me closer, whispering sweet prayers into my ear while holding me tightly, filled with gratitude for Allah.

I admired the movement of his lips as he prayed, feeling the warmth of his devotion. "You never forget," I said, hugging him tighter.

"How could I? He gave me everything, and today, with you beside me, my heart overflows with thankfulness."

"So, you've checked everything off your wishlist?" I asked, excitement bubbling within me.

"No, not everything, begum jaan."

"Does she know?"

To escape his hold, I tickled him, and to my surprise, he jumped as if a squirrel had scurried by.

"Anything but tickles!" He exclaimed, darting away from me.

"What! Are you ticklish?" I giggled, pursuing him with more tickles. But before I could launch another attack, he trapped my arms, intertwining my legs, leaving me unable to escape while he could tease me at his will.

"What are you doing?" I asked, my cheeks flushed with shyness.

"I'm preparing my morning coffee," he replied, inching closer. "What?" I said, bewildered by his intent.

"Irtaka," I murmured, catching sight of that mischievous smile. "What's cooking up?"

"I'm going to teach you how to brew my favorite morning coffee."

He loosened his grip on one arm, caressing my face and gently closing my eyes.

"First, you must recognize the fragrance of the coffee beans." He inhaled deeply, drawing in my scent, causing me to blush. "Then, feel the bean with your fingers." His touch ignited a fire within me, intoxicating and irresistible.

"Now, pour the coffee beans into the grinder." He held me close, and I felt his passion envelop me.

"It's time to savor the aroma of the ground coffee." We breathed each other in, lost in the moment.

"Now pour the coffee into the cup and relish the sips." As he spoke, he began kissing me, having completed his coffee-making ritual. I was utterly captivated by his vibrant energy; his loving embrace and masculine scent were the cherry atop our shared bliss.

The kisses began soft and gentle, but soon grew fervent as he savored his cup of love. I longed for him to drink me in, but he played coy, merely sipping, teasing, and igniting my desires. He had already etched himself into my heart long before our confessions, but now he had marked me, and I surrendered to him willingly.

Irtaka locked eyes with me, his gaze intense. "You are all mine, baby. I love you so much."

"I'm all yours. I love you too," I whispered, kissing him tenderly on his neck.

He held me with a knowing look as he moved slowly, and together we savored our coffee, lazily snuggling in bed.

"Don't we have work today?" I asked, nudging him aside as I sat up.

"No, you're not well, so we're on vacation!" He proclaimed with a broad smile.

"Really! A vacation! We have the orphanage project to tackle, Irtaka. I feel better now; we can surely work." I replied, feeling a twinge of insecurity. "Does Alia know about us?"

"No one knows but us, Tanisha," he answered, his smile reassuring.

"But Alia has spy talents," I warned, raising an eyebrow.

"Spy talents?" He echoed, intrigued.

"Yes, she can sense our feelings even before we do. She has an uncanny ability to read people."

"Well, she is intelligent!" He laughed. "Smarter than us, I must say!"

"I knew exactly what I felt for you from day one, Miss Tanisha."

"Then why didn't you say anything, Irtaka?" I turned my back to him, feigning annoyance.

"I promised to let you be certain of your choices, to ensure your love was genuine, and to wait," he murmured, hugging me from behind, resting his chin on my shoulder.

"Promised whom?" I asked, playing with his beard.

"Myself!" He said after a long pause, "Alia is sharp; she'll figure it out soon," he said, kissing my cheek softly and pulling me closer

"Will she tell?" I asked, worry creeping in.

"Are you worried she'll spill the beans and that people won't approve? Or are you concerned about me? Do you think I want to keep this hidden?" He replied, turning me to face him.

How does he read my mind and articulate my fears?

"What! No, I mean, I don't know how this all will affect you and your life. People have their biases about inter-religious love and other matters."

"Other matters! What do you mean?" He pressed.

"Yeah, I mean the marriage part," noticed the teasing smirk on his face.

"I'm not worried about them. I'm worried about you! Are you sure you want this?" I asked with my trembling voice and uncertainty.

Irtaka turned me towards him and lifted my chin. "Tanisha, I love you. I am certain about us with every fiber of my being! We are meant to be together forever. Their opinions will not dictate my choices." He gazed into my eyes, leaned in, smiled, and kissed me with all his love.

"Can we go to the office?" I suggested, eager to shift the conversation.

"Of course!" He replied, lifting me into his arms and planting a passionate kiss on my forehead, as if I were the most precious treasure in his life. I could feel his heartbeat quicken as I rested my head against his bare chest.

"I'll just run home, freshen up, and pick you up in an hour, my love; get ready by then," he said, kissing me goodbye on the lips.

After a delightful breakfast, we drove to the office, but an uneasy feeling settled in my stomach, a foreboding sense that something was amiss. Irtaka's hand rested on my lap, pulling me back to the present.

"There will come a time far in the future when we'll be grandparents, sitting in the back seat of a car, holding hands while our grandchildren giggle in the front," he promised. "I vow to support and love you forever; I promise you eternity, my love."

He smiled as he spoke, and I squeezed his hand in return, sharing a silent moment of joy.

Upon entering the office building together, I felt a mix of familiarity and anticipation, wishing for this day to be unique. Yet, I struggled to find the courage to express my feelings.

Thud! I fell , twisting my ankle. Irtaka, a few steps behind, lunged forward to catch me. "Woah! What a memorable entry of love!" I chuckled uncontrollably.

"What?" He asked, puzzled.

"I thought it would be romantic, given that this will be our first time coming to the office after..."

"Oh, you mean after our morning coffee!" He teased.

"No," I blushed .

"Let me help you," he said, scooping me into his arms and stepping into the lift. "What are you doing?" I exclaimed in astonishment.

"Making it memorable forever!" He declared with a grin.

"And also announcing to the world that we're in love," I added, feigning annoyance.

"Aren't we?" He asked, leaning in for a kiss.

As the lift doors opened, we were greeted by Alia. "Hi!" She exclaimed, her eyes wide with surprise.

"She needs first aid," Irtaka said, gesturing for Alia to fetch some supplies. "Yes, Bhai Jaan!" She replied, rushing toward her desk.

Everyone in the office eyed us, yet remained silent.

Irtaka gently helped me into his chair and began applying balm to my ankle. "What now? Do I get candy?" I joked.

"Of course, you do!" He said, producing a gift-wrapped box.

The box reminded me of the red velvet one from yesterday. My heart raced with suspicion.

"What is it now? I've already taken my medicine."

He grinned his mischievous smile. "Open it!" He urged, eagerly awaiting my reaction.

I tore off the wrapping, and to my shock, I found a paperweight engraved with "IT."

I stared at it, bewildered. "IT! What does it mean?" I looked shocked rather than amused.

"When the time is right, I promise I will tell you, but till then, we can play the guessing game." He said and smirked. The first thing that popped into my mind was "Irtaka and Tanisha," but I knew it was deeply connected to something before we met. "I can see your angry, confused face!" He rolled my chair behind the book rack and kissed my lips.

"That's not fair. It's 2:0! You took kisses for yourself, and I got none; besides, we are in the office." I could not stop but blush thinking about how much he loved me. "Don't you have any work?"

"Yea, I was about to ask the same question, Tanisha, don't you have any work?" He laughed.

I opened my mouth but said nothing. I got up to get going, but instead, he pulled me in his arms and started kissing me. I returned the favor and looked at him; he enjoyed every part and let his emotions flow.

"Irtaka, someone will see us; it's inappropriate," I said, pushing him away.

He hugged me tightly for once and then stepped back. I knew exactly what he felt because I too wanted to be in his arms, kiss and love him.

"I'll cook tonight." He said like a master chef.

"Umm! I am a fan of your coffee I had this morning," and he blushed. It was one of the rare moments which I had witnessed.

A masculine Arabic handsome hunk blushing out of love, I was undone again by his mere expressions; I hugged him and kissed his blushing cheeks.

"So, you need office coffee?" He asked, coming forward to kiss me again.

"Irtaka's testosterone."

"What!"

"Guesswork?"

"Keep guessing, testosterone," he said, rolling his eyes.

"You should go and work from my cabin today before we do something crazy," I said, pushing him away.

As he walked out, I saw Alia waiting at the door with flowers in her hand. She had a glee in her eyes, and I knew she knew.

"Hi, Alia!" I smiled.

"Hello, Miss Tanisha! How are you?" She said while passing the white tulips to me.

"I'm pretty good now." I could see her eyes asking me several questions. "May you please update me on the orphanage project, Alia," I said as I preferred to ignore the topic.

"Yes, Miss Tanisha, I'll be back with the file from your cabin, as you would love to sit here for a while," she said, sounding excited.

I could sense the happiness in her voice, "Yes, Alia, I'll work from Mr. Irtaka's cabin for now." I sat there smiling and rewinding all the beautiful moments since last night.

She returned, running with fear all over her face as if she had seen a ghost.

"Fire, " she said in a panicked voice. The building was on fire, and we needed to evacuate. Irtaka also entered the cabin behind her.

We both looked grave for a second; I was still analyzing the shocking news when Irtaka held my hand and pulled Alia with his other hand, taking us out of his cabin.

"Go down the stairs and be safe," he gestured for Alia and me to lead the ladies down the stairways.

He was worried about others and ran across the room to help them safely reach the stairways as the small fire turned into flames.

The panic was widespread; shouts of names and the heat of the fire just made it difficult to think of anything. I exited the gate, came to an open area, and saw smoke. It was just a window, but in no time, we could see flames.

People were all gathered, and gradually, the numbers were increasing, but no one could do anything.

The fire workers arrived, and the truck entered the gate but stopped at a point. The lobby was not designed to take that kind of weight, and thus, they could not extinguish the fire from the ground or with the help of ladders. The office building is not a skyscraper, but still, ten floors were high.

Firefighters started pulling people out. I waited a minute but could not stop running up the stairways. I heard people calling my name, but I could not stop with the thought of him inside the building, blazing in the fire.

Irtaka! I entered the hall and could not see anything, nor could I see anyone, but a hand on my shoulder made me turn. Mr. Ibrahim was out of breath.

"Let me help you, please, Mr. Ibrahim. Come this way?"

"My granddaughter, Sara!" He exclaimed in worry. "What? Where?" I asked, highly shocked.

"I asked her to wait in Alia's cabin," he said, tears of fear emerging.

"Don't worry; I'll go get her. You try to go down by the stairs." And I ran amidst the flames and smoke as I enter Alia's office area.

"Sara! Come here, please!" She sat there under the desk, "Come baby." She was scared and did not understand a word I said.

"Taeal 'iilaa huna min fadlik' iinaa Khayif

Hubibi' ana huna min ajlak, Taeal' iilaa huna min fadlik." I said in Arabic so that she could understand what I was trying to say.

"Tanisha! Take my coat." Mr. Ibrahim threw his coat towards me.

I covered myself with a coat and ran towards Sara, with the flames rising. I covered Sara with the coat, but coming back seemed impossible.

I heard glass shatter, to my relief. It was Irtaka with the firefighters.

"Stay down! Stay down"! He gestured, and in a moment, the water jet extinguishers were used in our direction. Irtaka ran towards us and took us in his arms; I felt safe. We stood there while the firefighters were extinguishing the fire.

"What were you thinking, Tanisha? What were you thinking?" He stared at me with anger. "Sir, we need you to evacuate the building." One of the firefighters said.

He took Sara in one arm and me in the other, and we ran towards the exit, saving ourselves from all the flames. We met Mr. Ibrahim in the open ground, and Sara ran towards him.

Doctors and nurses helped people who were injured.

"Alia! Are you okay?" I asked, hugging Alia in relief.

"Yes, Miss Tanisha! Are you okay?" She said in a concerned tone.

"Yeah, I'm fine. Did anyone get hurt?" I asked, looking towards the employees.

"No, but they are in shock. Don't worry, Miss Tanisha; everything will be fine," she said with a faint, reassuring smile.

I saw Irtaka talking to the police about how the fire started.

He came and held my hand. I hesitated a bit because I was well aware that PDA moments are not readily accepted in Dubai.

"I need to go home, something urgent." He said in a severe tone.

"Is Dad okay?" I asked, unable to understand what had happened to him suddenly.

"Yeah, he is good, but I must be home. I'll drop you home on my way. Come," he said, gesturing for me to move towards the car.

I just nodded, knowing it wasn't the right time to ask questions.

"Alia, will you please stay with Tanisha?" "Ji! Bhai Jaan."

While we drove, I saw his jawline clinching; I sensed he was worried about something. "Irtaka, is there something you are hiding from me?" I asked, consistently looking towards him. "Nothing to worry about, Tanisha; you need to rest. You are not well."

"What is troubling you?" I said, trying to talk him out.

"Nothing is troubling me. Everyone is fine, and the fire is under control," he said calmly.

"Are you okay"? I asked in a concerned tone.

He said nothing but nodded positively. "Everything is fine," he declared, looking in the rare view mirror.

I saw a security van arriving at the gates of my bungalow.

"You both stay in the bungalow; please stay in and don't go anywhere. I'll be back in a few hours." He said as he dropped us at the door.

I was worried for him; it was difficult to see him this disturbed. Alia kept her hand on my shoulder and gave me a reassuring look. We smiled faintly at each other and moved inside the house.

CHAPTER 14

I sank into the couch, my head bowed low, cradled between my palms as the events of the day's turmoil replayed in my mind. Just then, Alia entered, bearing two cups of steaming hot coffee, a delightful assortment of cookies, and her ever-blooming smile.

"Miss Tanisha, you haven't had a morsel since morning; you must eat something," she said, gracefully setting the tray upon the table before settling next to me. With a gentle touch, she placed her hand on my shoulder, embracing me sideways while soothingly rubbing my back.

"I'm okay, Alia, truly. No need to fret," I assured her, returning her embrace with warmth.

"These pictures are so beautiful," she said, trying to change the topic.

"After my parents passed away, it was difficult." My sister played a significant role in taking responsibility and caring for us. I sipped my coffee, and my thoughts instantly shifted to Vinayak. Vinayak, on the other hand, acts as the eldest and the smartest amongst us despite being the youngest one."

"It feels so good to hear about your siblings," she said, trying to help me lift my mood.

"I still remember one time Mom and Kaashvi did not allow me to eat pizza, and I had locked myself in my room; Vinayak sat on the window to talk to me and cracked jokes and promised to take me on the world tour where we would eat ice creams and pizzas till we dropped."

Alia carefully listened to me with her smile. "You are lucky to have Kaashvi, Vinayak, and Bhaijaan in your life."

"I am happy to have you too, Alia!" I said, and she smiled.

"Has Vinayak always been a great observer and can read people's minds like I do?" She asked.

"Yes, Alia," I told her stories about how Vinayak would prank his class and the major incident when he convinced his class to make airplanes out of their final answer sheets and fly them.

Alia gazed at me in disbelief, yet her focus was unwavering. I could sense the thrill in her voice each time we delved into Vinayak's subject, and before I could spiral into contemplation, I cast those thoughts aside. As the night deepened, I urged Alia to sleep in my bedroom. A heavy heart weighed upon me for Vinayak, prompting me to reach for my phone, yearning to give him a call.

"Tanisha," my heart sank when I heard his voice. I wanted to cry.

"How are you?" I said in a meek voice.

"I'm great as ever; what's up with you?" He said in his charming voice.

"I'm good. When are your exams finishing?" I enquired.

"I'm already done with them! how's your health?" He questioned in a concerned tone.

"I'm feeling much better," I said

"It doesn't seem so; you sound low. Is everything all right?" He asked and paused for a minute,

I wanted to cry my heart out but kept quiet. "I'm fine; I'm just feeling a little sluggish. So, when are you coming to Dubai?" I said in an attempt to divert my mind.

"I'm planning to come next week to Thank Mr. Irtaka in person; Kaashvi told me how he accompanied you to the hospital while taking good care of you," he said sarcastically.

"Have you booked the tickets?" I asked, dodging Irtaka's topic. I kept silent and said nothing, "He is important, Vinayak," and said nothing more.

"You seem hesitant to talk about him over the call, so I don't analyze him till I meet him in person." He said sternly. "I know he took great care of you while staying beside you in the hour of need. I can sense that even he reciprocates the same feelings as you."

I was dumbstruck, but somehow, I knew he would figure it out without my intervention. "Vinayak! He is important," I said again, worried about his reaction.

"Don't worry, whatever you choose, but I have concerns about him, and I have all the rights to question and know him before I agree. And you aren't even aware of the world around you."

"Enlighten me about the world around me!" I was feeling a bit edgy about the conversation now.

You cannot be naive to believe there does not exist any love Jihad," he said sternly.

"What!" I said in a shocked tone. "Vinayak, you cannot be serious."

"You have to understand there is a parallel hate world around us," and he disconnected the call angrily.

I knew Vinayak very well. He would stand beside me even if I were wrong, but he would also painfully grill me to ensure I was making the right decision.

I knew what love jihad meant; Mom had spent all her life proving love jihad as a tool of West to alienate the Islamic community. The theory itself was Western.

"Love Jihad," I took a deep breath and typed it into a search engine.

Love Jihad is an alleged activity where the youth of a particular religion utilize emotional appeals or charm to entice girls into the conversation by feigning love. Wikipedia read.

Seriously! I thought to stay focused and kept on reading. The concept originated in 2009 in southern India.

Yeah, obviously India has to come up with such stuff.

As I scrolled down, I saw an interview with the girl who was the victim of jihad love; she was lured into a trap by a boy from another community who pretended to love her. It all started with friendship, and slowly, they began dating; the inter-religious relationship was unacceptable to the family. They ran away from the village, but the boy returned to his family after two days and asked her to convert to Islam if she wanted to be with him. She had no option as she had left her home to run away with him, and then the actual abuse started.

There were interviews of the victims and their families; I opened several tabs, and after every click, a new world of hatred unfolded. It was disgusting to read because the words that were used to describe the heinous crime were themselves cruel.

The articles, at length, described the flagitious acts of the people in torturing the victims. It contained the data on the number of conversions every year.

Articles and interviews were just the start. I surfed various Facebook and Instagram pages and was astonished to see people crazy over their religion, and women were just objects to them. Objectifying and treating them as a breeder is insane, and what do these men think of them?

I could relate to Vinayak's fear. After reading Love Jihad, I knew he was sacred for me on a whole new level. I was shattered. I tried to reason with myself; maybe the above-said things were an example of immature love being targeted by political issues, high-level beneficiaries, or bad people.

I did not know what to do; I just could not relate to the victim because I could not imagine Irtaka's wrong side, nor did I want to. I liked to believe he was a nice person and loved me honestly.

But the seed was planted. I was scared but also loved Irtaka immensely; I could not accept that if any of this were accurate, he would harm me in any way.

I have always believed love is a pure, selfless feeling. When people are in love, they can give up everything and do anything for each other. Nothing in the world can pollute the relationship of pure love.

But whatever I was reading said otherwise about people. Love was a mere weapon for them; how could they pretend to have pure feelings? How can anyone force someone in love? I went on reading, surfing the net, stumbling upon articles that portrayed poor girls being victims of prostitution in jihad love. I thought I misunderstood the article or something might be wrong with the language. I scrolled down, and to my horror, I found horrible comments by people who were ready to slit each other's throats. They accused each other in every inhuman way they could. How can these people talk about love when they are not even aware of the word human behavior? How can these people feel love emotions with so much hatred in their minds? I took a deep breath, not knowing where Irtaka and I were standing with so many uncertainties. I had my fears, and he might have them too; we have to fight them together, but will he?

Thoughts about all the text and comments I had just read ran through my mind. My fear shouted back at me, telling me I was stuck and had to be careful. What if it's all true, and I am just a victim of all this façade? Shit man! I was screwed big time.

I wanted to believe all this was a lie. Still, the intensity of the people commenting on the web pages and the way the media had brought it in front, I felt it all-natural, but Irtaka's eyes, his face, and his concern all came to my mind, telling me to believe in love. All those feelings cannot be false. I was so engrossed in shitting ideas I held my hair with my hands, trying to stop my thoughts. I wish it could help, but nothing did help. I was getting scared every minute and had no idea of my next course of action. I sat on the couch, praying that whatever I read was not true between Irtaka and I. . I had faith and tried to convince my inner self that he was different and that we would be different with each passing moment.

I was lost in my thoughts when Alia came in; she switched on the lights and sat beside me, a bit sleepy.

I raised my head to observe the growing darkness outside and this beautiful human being beside me; at this moment, I couldn't have been more thankful to God for gifting me with such amazing people.

"What happened, Miss Tanisha? You look worried?" She said, looking outside as the night grew darker.

"I was speaking to Vinayak, my younger brother. He will visit Dubai in a few days." "That's excellent news. What's worrying you?" She asked.

The doorbell rang, and Alia got up instantly to open the door.

"Bhai Jaan, how are you," she asked. Irtaka nodded positively and looked at me across the hall. "Let the driver drop you home; Abu must be waiting for you."

"Ji Bhai Jaan," Alia walked to me, smiled, and hugged me. "Alla Hafiz, Miss Tanisha."

"Bye, Alia."

As soon as Alia left the house, closing the door behind her, I looked towards Irtaka. He came closer to me, hugging me with all his might. He kissed my forehead and whispered, "I missed you."

"I missed you too," I said, looking into his eyes. It felt like my wait had taken my life, and now everything would be all right with Irtaka at my side.

He took me in his arms while we cuddled in one corner of the couch; his embrace felt like soothing ointment to my burned emotions. I preferred not to tell him about the fears.

Instead, I just wanted to listen to whatever he offered to say; his words were like the calm to the storm of my life.

"Irtaka," I whispered,

"Yes, my love," he said, lightly kissing my forehead. "What if your father or family doesn't approve of us?"

He pulled me at arm's length and embraced me again in his strong arms.

"Don't worry about anyone; you are a lovely person. Abu and everyone else will love you. Alia loves you," he said, looking down at me and brushing my hair aside.

"Irtaka, you realize that there are far-stretched differences between us, our religion, our society. How will we ever be able to make everyone happy?" I hugged him tightly; my question scared the hell out of me.

He said, "By focusing on ourselves and our happiness," tightening his grip on me while kissing my hair.

I sobbed out of fear and sniffled in his arms.

"I love you, Tanisha. You are mine, and I am all yours." He kept caressing my back. "We have numerous differences, but I promise a beautiful life ahead." I rested my head on his chest and wondered what that beautiful life would look like.

"Irtaka, I will do whatever it takes to make us work. I will convert!" I knew I was contradicting my own beliefs and ideologies. Why was I making promises that I wouldn't keep? I was lying to Irtaka and giving him false hopes; I was already cheating his heart, maybe because I was madly in love with him.

"Wait, what?" He brought me before him; his eyes widened as he gave me a grave look. "No, you don't have to convert Tanisha. I want you to be the same person I fell in love with; no modifications needed. You are unique from the crowd. This is what made me fall head over heels for you." He paused, took my hands in his, cleared his throat and continued in a lower, intense tone," I do not want you to change your religion or even the tiniest bit about you, ever in our lives. Love me the way you do and stay by my side forever. I love you." He took me in his arms again.

I cried my fear out and sobbed; I was in the arms of Mr. Irtaka Ali Khan, a Muslim with whom I had fallen in love and who was madly in love with me. He did not want to convert me.

I looked up and poked his face with my finger to check that I was not dreaming.

"You are not dreaming, begum jaan! And that hurts." He made a face to make me smile, and looking deep into my eyes, he said, "Tanisha, I am sure by every word I say I adore you the way you are. I promise to safeguard your freedom, thoughts, and happiness and stand by your side forever. Wear your sparkling smile and those twinkling eyes each day for the rest of my life."

"Can I ask you one question?" I said, playing with his hair.

"Sure, begum jaan." He said with a broad smile. I blushed, hearing the words he used to address me.

"How are you so different?" He raised his eyebrows in a perfect arc and slightly blushed. "Now, is that a compliment or a comment?"

I looked into his eyes and felt ashamed of my earlier thoughts. How could I accuse Irtaka? A person who is stripping down his emotions, he cares for me, my lifestyle, and my freedom. How could I ever think in my wildest dreams that his love might be a jihad love? "Umm, actually, it's a compliment. I have never seen a guy like you. I never saw a person of this intellect and thoughts," I said, trying to hide my embarrassment.

"Hmmm," he said and closed his eyes. We clasped each other in a warm hug. "I need to tell you something?" And pulled away.

"What is it? He said, opening his eyes.

"Vinayak, my brother, is coming to Dubai, and he knows about us!"

His eyes were happy, but he was searching mine, which were not reciprocating the same feeling, I could sense the thunderstorm coming!

"What is the concern, Tanisha?" He said, looking me in the eye.

"I doubt he approves of our relationship," I said with fear in my eyes.

"Don't worry. We will do our best to win him on our side," he said, pressing my hands lightly. "You don't know him, Irtaka," I said with fear.

"I just know one thing: I am in love with you, and he loves you too. Love is an unconditional conditioner for all hard feelings."

I just took a deep breath and hugged him, "You have to win him, please." "I will," he said and tightened the hug.

CHAPTER 15

As I stood in anticipation for Vinayak at Dubai Airport, my mind danced with logical arguments to sway his heart. Irtaka's perceptive deemed it unnecessary to my growing unease as Vinayak's arrival neared. He remained a silent guardian, brewing coffee and conjuring meals to uplift my spirits.

"Give him time; he will come around," Irtaka's reassuring mantra echoed within me.

Then, like a scene from a cherished dream, I spotted Vinayak, his suitcase in tow, traversing the hall towards me. He approached, set his bags down, and enveloped me in a warm embrace.

"I missed you so much!" I exclaimed, holding him close, my toes barely grazing the ground to reach his height.

"I missed you too," he replied, playfully tugging at my braid, his signature gesture. He leaned back, a glint of mischief in his eyes. "Are you here alone? I thought Mr. Irtaka would come to greet me," he remarked with a touch of sarcasm.

"Hahaha, very funny! Roast me as much as you like," I chuckled, brushing off his jest.

"Forget the roasting; I'm here to give you a good grilling, and you'll thank me for it later," he declared with unwavering confidence.

Understanding his protective brotherly intent, I simply returned his smile, feeling the warmth of our bond.

"So, what culinary delights are you conjuring today for me?" Vinayak inquired, lifting his bags with a playful flourish.

"I thought you came to visit your ailing sister!" I retorted with a hint of sarcasm. "Ah, I see! It's love you're suffering over," he teased, a smirk dancing on his lips.

"Will you cease this nonsense?" I shot him an annoyed glance.

"We dine out; Irtaka shall join us." I swung the car door shut and caught sight of his exasperated expression.

"You have feelings for him?" He fixed his gaze upon me, and I remained silent. After a thoughtful pause, I finally murmured, "He is different."

His smiled and radiated that familiar brotherly warmth. The cab fell into a comfortable hush, yet I sensed his concern lingering in the air.

As I peered out the window, the sunbaked roads of Dubai unfurled beneath the gleaming white skyscrapers and drifting clouds.

In the kitchen, I stood at the counter, eagerly awaiting Irtaka's arrival. Vinayak lounged on the sofa, lost in the pages of a book, clad in his jeans and beloved black T-shirt. His tousled hair sparked memories of Mom's playful meddling with his style before outings. An avid reader, he often immersed himself in the realms of psychology and personal growth.

When Irtaka arrived, he was resplendent in a black Pathani suit, his beard neatly trimmed, hair impeccably styled, and that charming dimpled smile gracing his soft pink lips. I longed to kiss him, but it seemed he had plans with my brother today; I stood, a silent observer to their first encounter.

They faced each other, a moment suspended in silence, gazing into one another's eyes.

"Hey Vinayak," Irtaka extended his hand in greeting. "How are you? How was your flight?" His voice was warm and inviting.

"I'm well, and the flight was fine," Vinayak replied in a rather lackluster tone, offering a fleeting smile. Their hands clasped, and Irtaka turned to me. "What do you think about 'Beachcombers' for tonight?"

"Absolutely! It's perfect for those loud, awkward exchanges," I thought with a hint of sarcasm. I didn't expect Vinayak to warm up to Irtaka right away, but I hoped for a budding camaraderie.

This beachfront sanctuary promised tantalizing pan-Asian dishes and breathtaking views of the iconic Burj Al Arab and welcoming water fronts

As we stepped into the open dining area, the opulent blend of glass and wood captivated my senses; the gentle strains of a live band filled the air with melodious Arabic tunes, while couples strolled along the shore, reveling in the enchanting evening. We settled at a beautifully set wooden table, the beach's embrace surrounding us; Vinayak and Irtaka now faced each other.

"I've heard so much about you; I was excited to finally meet," Irtaka said, attempting to break the ice and lighten the atmosphere.

"Lucky you!" Vinayak retorted, his tone dripping with sarcasm. I glanced at Irtaka, who seemed slightly taken aback by my younger sibling's demeanor, yet his smile remained reassuring.

Across the table, they sat in a silent standoff, their gazes locking as if they were engaged in a conversation within a realm unseen.

"I will have pork," Vinayak declared, gazing intently into Irtaka's eyes.

"Vinayak, are you out of your mind?" I implored, my hands pressed firmly on the table, striving to instill some reason.

"Okay then, I will have beef!" Irtaka countered, his gaze unwavering.

"O, God!" I buried my face in my hands. "Please don't do this," I pleaded. The urge to flee clawed at me, yet I knew that leaving dynamite near a blazing fire would only invite chaos, so I chose to endure this tempest.

Vinayak questioned sharply, "What if my sister is under the delusion that she loves you?" "What am I, six?" I interjected.

"I have and will give her all the time and space she needs to discern her feelings for me," Irtaka replied, dismissing my concern.

"What if she outshines you in success?" He asked with a hint of pride.

"I will ensure that comes to pass!" Irtaka declared, and a smile graced my lips.

"What if she doesn't want a baby?" Vinayak posed, my jaw dropping at the audacity of the question.

"Then so be it, for her happiness is my true desire," Irtaka responded with unwavering conviction.

"What if you find yourselves in conflict?"

"I would listen to her every word and seek harmony between us."

"What if you cause her pain, or she sheds tears because of you?"

"I could never bear to see her cry; the very thought of hurting her, even in a dream, is unbearable," Irtaka said, locking his gaze onto mine.

"Huh! As you say!" Vinayak scoffed, his annoyance evident as he disregarded Irtaka's sincerity.

"What troubles you, Vinayak?" Irtaka spoke, his voice touched with sorrow.

"I have my doubts about you," Vinayak replied bluntly.

"You don't know me! Not in the slightest!" Irtaka retorted, a fire igniting in his words.

"Exactly! That's the heart of the issue."

"I'm suspicious about why you like my sister. She is different, unlike girls in your community. Why do you wish to marry her? She doesn't even belong to your religion! Why marry a Hindu and then ask her to convert? Why don't you find one of your own? How can I not believe that you loving her will not be a part of some Jihad Love conspiracy?" Vinayak said, bursting in anger.

"What?" Irtaka said in a shocked state. He looked at me with disappointment as if this question had pierced his heart.

"Love Jihad"

I hid my face with my hands, knowing where all this led. I was witnessing something which would become a story for my grandkids or the sparks that would turn into a blazing fire and burn my happiness into ashes.

"Why would you think my love for your sister is jihadi?" Irtaka said, keeping a hand on the table and leaning forward.

"Because I don't know you, and you are too good to be true!" Vinayak said, raising his shoulders in disagreement.

"So, if I were a problematic man, would you agree to our relationship?"

"Then I wouldn't let you be anywhere near her."

"Vinayak, I love her, and I wish to marry her," Irtaka said, trying to convince him for the last time.

"And then ask her to convert!" Vinayak added, "Then the real problem will start. You will begin to change her, and if she does not do as you say, there will be friction between you both, and then you will abuse and torture her."

"You are not worried about her, but you are paranoid about me, and I can't help you if you don't let me explain myself to you. If you think this love and religion is my way, let's do it your way!" Irtaka snarled. I was anxious about where this conversation was going and wished everything to end as soon as possible.

"My way," Vinayak looked at him questioningly.

"Yes, you might be comfortable if everything happened as per your rules."

"Spend some time with me, see my lifestyle and everything that I do and then give your approval. Till then, I will not even cross paths with your sister. The day you approve our relationship is when I'll look at her. And as a brother, you have every right to do so. Be with me, judge me, read me, and then decide whether I am suitable for your sister. I will respect your decision; it may or may not be in our favor."

I could not help but observe the reaction of these two men fighting for my happiness.

Vinayak looked at me long enough; he took a deep breath, exhaled the air and agreed with a nod.

I stood up and walked away to the beach to leave them alone; the sand under my feet made a slip every time I stepped in it. My life seemed to slip from my hands whenever I tried to hold on to it.

"I am sorry," Vinayak said as he walked beside me. "After Mom and Dad, it is my responsibility to ensure you are safe, and I am just ensuring your happiness," Vinayak said in a low voice. He held my hand. "Trust me, Tanisha; this is necessary."

I looked at him and how big he had grown in such little time; I brushed his hair and smiled. I then glanced at Irtaka, who sat across the beach, smiling at us. His smile was very reassuring, telling me he could convince Vinayak.

We walked back. I smiled, looking at the vegan food served on the table. Irtaka had ordered my favorites with starters. Irtaka and Vinayak were hardcore vegetarians. They would not eat eggs, let alone beef or pork.

"Irtaka and I have decided to take a road trip in the morning." He said, looking at me with all his sincerity.

I looked up at Vinayak and then at Irtaka but said nothing. I could not stop thinking and recalling about a few minutes earlier; they wanted to kill each other, and now they like to go on a road trip.

"Mr. Irtaka will not come near you until I permit." Vinayak winked at me, and his notorious side was finally back, and I was relieved.

The following day, I entered the office. Irtaka wanted me back in the office when the renovations were done, but I could not sit at home all day. I needed a distraction from thinking about Irtaka and Vinayak and how they would get along. I was scared and regretful about not accompanying them.

The orphanage project was in full swing, and I knew I had to get my head straight for it. I slowly moved towards my cabin and looked around, nodding greetings. Alia, as usual, was holding up her smile.

"How long before we can open the office again," I asked Alia, who was fidgeting with some files on her desk.

"The painting will take a week, and also, the final touch with furniture will take another week." Alia said without looking at me; she had been struggling with police investigations and office renovations for a while now.

"I'll get the furniture ordered, so I need to finalize them by afternoon," she said and excused herself.

I sat in the corner of my cabin, staring at the wrecks left by the fire. My phone beeped, and a message from Irtaka popped.

"I love you. You are my strength."

CHAPTER 16

"My love for your sister is not Jihadi," Irtaka said in a calm voice while driving. "Your sister chooses to believe in the goodness of people just like your mother. Yes, we are incredibly different, but Vinayak, I have fallen in love with those differences. He said, trying to win my confidence.

"Mr. Irtaka, my sister believes love jihad is a myth; my mother thought the same, and she spent her whole life proving it, but her opinion differed on the last day of her life. I can guarantee you one thing: my mother would have reacted in the same manner if she had been here," Vinayak said in an annoyed tone.

After the long silence, Irtaka said in a hurtful voice," She proved Love jihad is a Western theory that misleads the world. Your mother was a great lover of humanity, Vinayak. She believed in peace and was a spokesperson for the people without a voice. She helped many Muslim boys and Girls from the weaker section of the society in building their lives.

"The way you speak about my mother, I assume you knew her well." Vinayak looked out the window, in no mood to discuss anything further.

"Yes, I knew her well because I was her student."

Vinayak ignored him and said nothing. "What else do you know about her?" He questioned, still looking out the window.

"I knew her enough to say one thing: that she loved her kids and wanted a safer world for them."

"Safer world! Mr. Irtaka." Vinayak looked at him this time fuming with anger

"Vinayak, the world still has humanity left!" Irtaka tried to reason with him.

"She was murdered by the people she stood up for," Mr Irtaka. Vinayak shouted at the top of his voice, frustrated with fear, do you even know what had happened to them.

Tires screeched as Irtaka applied the brakes to look at Vinayak.

Vinayak opened the car door, walked up the road for a minute, and then sat on the side of the way. He was shivering with anger and hate..

Irtaka slowly joined me without any words and waited for me to say something," She was murdered, Irtaka, by the people she was standing for."

"Why would you even say that, Vinayak? It was an accident!"

"Accident was a cover-up! It was a cold-blooded murder; her throat was slit open, she died on the spot, and my father was mercilessly stabbed. Dad was taken to the hospital, where he fought for his life on a ventilator for a few days but still couldn't survive.

Hindus and Muslims have been in the fight for a very long time now. I am not against you, but I am scared for my sister, and I don't want her to endure any of those situations."

"Vinayak! Who told you that the accident was a cover-up?" Irtaka asked.

"My mother was invited to deliver a lecture on some theories. She looked tensed as if she had worked herself up the night earlier. Also, I could see she was busy the whole week as she made phone calls and set up meetings. I could not accompany her as I had my assignments to submit the next day. She was on a call when I heard her say, 'Love jihad is a weapon 'many times over the phone that day. She tried to convince some higher officials as those calls weren't traceable. She was anxious and disturbed this whole time, the same evening she was met with the accident. The accident was mercilessly covered; all the medical files were sealed, and the actual pieces of evidence were tampered with, while the 'postmortem report 'said that the slit on the throat was bruising from the accident. I'm sure we were forcefully made to believe it was an accident, but there was no explanation for how this happened!

Dad was driving himself that day; I knew he wasn't drunk, and it was a clear highway. Then how the hell did the accident occur?

I wouldn't say I like so much of the community you hail from because my mother dedicated her life to improving the experience of young Muslim boys and girls, and this is how she is rewarded.

Every single minute I talk to you, I try to reason with myself, why not blame you and your people for my parent's death." Vinayak fumed angrily; Irtaka said nothing but sat there staring afar.

After a prolonged silence, he said, "Vinayak, just hear me out now; it cannot be possible! I have assisted her in her research of Love Jihad theory; her beliefs proved that Love Jihad is a weapon that Westerners are using against Muslims to discredit them in the world. There were and still are many bureaucrats and politicians who would benefit from proving your mother wrong, and the best way they could do that was by silencing her.

Professor always said proving the Love Jihad theory wrong is significant, or else it will create a negative impact, and again, the whole world will boycott the Islamic faith. Love Jihad will be the new face of terrorism. She believed this hatred would be widespread, where the world would corner the Islamic faith, and believers would be bullied and traumatized.

I firmly believe she was proving that "Love Jihad theory was a weapon being used by the Westernworld", and this would only benefit the Islamic faith. Then why would any Muslim want her dead? Vinayak, I have assisted your mother with many research and theories. I was in India a week before their accident. And now I am worried about Tanisha's well-being!" Irtaka said in a low voice.

"What do you mean?" Vinayak asked.

"Someone tried to harm Tanisha!" He continued in a low voice.

"When?" Vinayak looked gravely.

"First Attempt was with Tanisha's car; it was tempered, but she was lucky and did not use her car that day. Instead, my father used it and met with an accident. Then, a week later, there was a fire incident in the office. It started in Tanisha's cabin as she was the direct target."

"How did the fire break?"

"A box was delivered for her like a parcel, but it was a timer with a fire initiator. Police narrowed it down to a hate group that has been targeting Indian Immigrants."

"This is purely an attack on an individual and not immigrants, and you say she is safe with you!" Vinayak scoffed, and he could see me getting extremely worried about her. "Did the police get anything other than hate groups?"

"They did have a theory." He said and looked at me.

"What theory?"

"Even the police believe that your parents did not die in the accident; they were murdered." There was a long pause between us.

"So, I was right! They were murdered." Vinayak said with a clenched jaw and looked at him in anger.

CHAPTER 17

We were back on the road, and Vinayak was lost in his thoughts. It was difficult for me to accept Professor's murder; I felt guilty.

"When I received the shocking news about the accident, I called Kaashvi to pay my condolences and wanted to know how you guys were holding up. Kaashvi told me that Tanisha was not coping well and that she would lock herself in your parent's room for hours and was slipping into depression."

Vinayak kept staring at me, wanting to ask many questions but waited. So, to waive his confusion, I started answering them without him asking, "Kaashvi and I met in college several times when she came to deliver lunch for your mom."

"Oh yes! You worked with my mother, knew Kaashvi, and love Tanisha. What else do I still need to know?" Vinayak seemed seriously annoyed.

"Kaashvi planned to bring Tanisha to Dubai," I said, completing my side of the story.

"Just as you wanted!" Vinayak scoffed.

"Yes, for a long time, I wanted to expand my company, and when Kaashvi requested that I make arrangements for Tanisha to work here, I seized the opportunity to develop my company, keep Tanisha close, and comfort her in any manner I could. She came to the office early for weeks and returned late as if she was punishing herself for something. We were terrified and worried about her.

I gathered my courage to ask her for coffee one day, and to my surprise, she agreed. It was difficult to see her in pain and not be able to talk to her, but I could not do anything about it."

"So, you and Kaashvi made plans, ugh! Did Kaashvi know about your feelings from the start?" He asked in an annoyed tone.

"Not until Tanisha was in the hospital. She figured out what I felt for her and was happy about it."

"Did mom approve of you two?" He looked at me in the eye.

"I would not have approached your sister if your mother had not approved of us. I confided in your mother about my feelings for Tanisha. She was delighted, but she wanted Tanisha to choose her life partner."

"Hence, I promised her I would always give Tanisha the time and freedom to fall in love with me."

"You had Mom's blessings; Kaashvi is on your side, and I am sure Dad also approved of you. Why wait and seek my blessings?" He said, highly pissed at the discoveries.

"Because it matters for Tanisha!" I said and raced the car.

We entered the office, and Vinayak saw people trying to retrieve what was burnt. He was horrified to see the place and looked at me in utter state of shock.

CHAPTER 18

Who would take such drastic measures as to set the office ablaze to harm Tanisha? How can she find safety in Dubai? Troubling thoughts flickered through my mind as I gazed at Irtaka.

"Vinayak, allow me to introduce Alia. She is my sister."

"Alia, this is Mr. Vinayak, Miss Tanisha's brother."

"Pleasure to meet you, Mr. Vinayak," she greeted with a charming smile.

"Please, just Vinayak. The pleasure is mine, Alia."

I found myself captivated by her as she conversed with Irtaka about those crucial files.

"Alia, could you kindly guide Vinayak to Tanisha's cabin? I have some pressing calls to attend to," Irtaka said, retrieving his phone and signaling for us to depart.

"Of course," she replied, her eyes meeting mine with a warm smile. "Mr. Vinayak, shall we?" I nodded, finding comfort in her presence amidst the chaos and uncertainty. As we walked through the bustling corridors of the office, I couldn't help but notice the way Alia navigated the space with ease and confidence. Her demeanor was reassuring, and I felt a sense of calm wash over me.

"Vinayak," she began softly, glancing over at me, "I know you must be worried about your sister. I assure you, we're doing everything we can to ensure her safety."

As we reached Tanisha's cabin, Alia paused and turned to face me. "Remember, if there's anything you need or if there's anything I can do to help, please don't hesitate to ask."

Her kindness was sincere, and I felt grateful for her support in this tumultuous time. "I will, Alia. Thank you."

With a gentle nod, she opened the door to Tanisha's cabin, and I stepped inside, feeling weighed down by the worries for Tanisha. I glanced around as she offered me a seat in Tanisha's cabin.

"Are you okay?" She asked, a little concerned.

"I guess."

"Coffee?"

"Nothing," I just sat there as if the weight of the world was on me.

"Do you want to talk about it?" She sat, looking deeply concerned. Her eyes expressed clearly, and she placed her hands on the table, looking straight at me, waiting.

"The fire in the office was meant to harm Tanisha."

"Irtaka Bhai Jaan is doing his best," she interrupted, reassuring me of her faith in him.

"But is my sister safe? Her safety is my concern."

"She is safe with Irtaka Bhai Jaan."

"How can you say this with confidence?"

"Because everyone is safe with him," She looked away into the distance. "I understand your worries, Mr. Vinayak. Miss Tanisha is fortunate to have two loving men who are so protective of her. Not every girl gets that!" She smiled and stood, looking at me.

"You're back," Tanisha said, entering the room.

"We're going out for coffee," I stood up and exclaimed.

"I would love to. I know a perfect Turkish place, but you'll have to wait," she said, looking at the files Alia had just placed.

"We are going for coffee," he stood behind Alia, smirking. "We were having quite a conversation before you entered, and I would love to continue it over coffee."

I smiled, looking at Alia, hoping she would agree.

CHAPTER 19

"How are you?" I asked, entering Irtaka's cabin. He did not respond, so I walked towards him and patted his back. He looked startled. "Is everything all right?" I asked, trying to read his mind.

"Yes, all good!" He said briefly. "How was the drive?" I asked.

Irtaka stood there, lost with no words, holding his phone tightly. "Irtaka?" I spoke louder to get his attention and waited for his response.

Irtaka forced a smile and instantly hugged me. "I love you, Tanisha, and I promise I will keep you safe and protected." There was fear in his voice, and his hug felt tight.

I did not say a word but hugged and caressed him back. I knew he was worried, and every day was challenging for us.

"So, what are the updates on the orphanage project?" Irtaka asked, changing the topic.

"The project is going as planned, and I have also asked Alia to visit the orphanage tomorrow to have the files finalized and fix the date for the Completion Party."

"That's great; by the way, where is Alia? I have been searching for her."

"Vinayak asked her for coffee," I said and smiled.

"Interesting!"

I could see the astonishment in his tone.

"Is it possible?" I looked at him.

"Let them run their race," he said, tightening his arms around me and kissing my forehead.

Alia and I stepped into the Menagerie café, where the royal blue and white walls danced with the glowing reflections of Monet prints, basking in the sun's golden embrace. The glass-fronted counter boasted an opulent display of cakes and confections. Soft jazz melodies floated through the air, while large windows and silver square tables adorned with delicate vases of pink lilies enhanced the café's inviting charm.

I could feel Alia's shyness radiate from her hesitant walk, as she averted her gaze. In her presence, I found solace; my heart thumped louder with each passing moment, drawn to her like a moth to a flame. Her grace enveloped her like an ethereal veil, captivating me in a manner unlike any before.

She selected a table on the sunlit terrace; I gently pulled out her chair. As she settled with an elegant poise, her eyes darted around, revealing a hint of trepidation.

"Is there something I can do to ease your discomfort?" I inquired, taking my seat across from her. "Why did you ask me out for coffee?" She replied, her voice a whisper.

"We can return if you wish!"

"No, breaking the formalities in this environment will be easier, " she said, smiling slightly.

"Now that you and I wish to achieve the same goal, I'd like to know what coffee you prefer."

"I prefer my coffee with good company." Alia smiled at the waiter and ordered, "Two Turkish coffees and two baklavas."

"May I ask you something?" I asked, glancing at her continuously all this while.

"Please, do." She said and waited for me to continue.

"What is it that hurts?" I asked with a warm expression on my face.

"Life that we endure, becomes pain and pleasure both." Her voice was cold and hurt. "How so?"

"You must endure pain to realize what love and peace mean in life."

"You are an introvert who drinks lots of water," I said, smirking.

Alia looked at me and then at her emptied water bottle.

"Yes, Dubai's heat is cruel if you are not hydrated," she said, adjusting her hijab.

"And what about the trusting people?" As I asked, she stopped and looked at me.

"Let's say I trust the people I know."

"Then why be introverted and deny yourself the freedom?"

"When salvation is freedom, you need not seek it elsewhere."

"But you do seek happiness in other's happiness."

"Yes, it gives me happiness, and I am sufficiently happy." She said, playing with the lilies in the vase.

"What does that even mean, "sufficiently happy?" I asked curiously.

"The right amount of happiness I require to continue my life." She said, looking at me sternly this time.

"There is no scale to measure happiness required, Ms. Alia. It is possible to learn how to be happy beyond measure." There was a momentary silence between us. I felt I overstepped this time but wanted to keep talking to her. "I'm sorry; I did get carried away a little with my words."

She didn't answer and continued to sip her coffee and eat her Baklava, which had arrived. We looked at each other in silence. She said a lot through her eyes. A gentle breeze rustled through the terrace, carrying with it the scent of fresh lilies and the rich aroma of Turkish coffee. It was a moment of unspoken understanding, a pause that allowed us both to reflect on the delicate threads of conversation we had woven.

As Alia set her cup down, a small smile played on her lips. "You know," she began softly, "it's rare to find someone who listens as intently as you do."

I returned her smile, grateful for the connection that seemed to be forming between us. "And it's rare to find someone who speaks with such depth and sincerity," I replied.

We spent the next few minutes enjoying our baklava, the sweet syrup mingling with the bitter notes of the coffee, creating a perfect harmony. The world around us seemed to slow down, as if the café itself recognized the significance of the moment we shared.

"I want to thank you," Alia said, breaking the silence, "For inviting me here. Sometimes, stepping out of one's comfort zone reveals unexpected joys."

I nodded, feeling a warmth spread through me. "And thank you," I said earnestly, "For trusting me with your thoughts. I hope this can be the beginning of many more conversations."

She chuckled, her eyes sparkling with a newfound ease. "Perhaps it will be," she said, as we both rose to leave.

"Have you been to Burj Khalifa?" She asked

"No, surely planning to visit someday," I said and continued sipping my coffee.

"Would you like to visit it tomorrow with me?" She asked, and I could feel the hesitation in her voice.

"As a date?" I played my chances this time.

"No, more like an assistant. I need someone to hold my files. I am visiting the orphanage, which is near Burj Khalifa." Alia smiled at me this time.

It will be an honor to assist you."

"You don't have someone in your life?" She asked shyly.

"How could I? You were in Dubai, hidden behind the files." I said and looked lovingly but flirtishly at her.

She blushed at my cheesy flirting, and the redness of her cheeks made her look all the more adorable.

"And why don't you have someone in your life?" I asked.

"No one is too eager to dig beneath the files," she said coldly and smiled, trying to hide the gushing pain.

"What is it?" I asked

"Nothing, just a few hiccups that leave you sublimed," she said, reaching for some tissues she had kept in her bag.

I said nothing but observed her dearly.

"I am sorry. It has been a while. And I have not talked so much to anyone in a long while. ," she said, lowering her head. "I was hurt long back, but the imprints haven't left since then, and every time I feel safe, happy, and positive, the imprints rewind through my eyes like a CD being played." Her voice was withered, and she felt deficient.

Why was I feeling emotionally connected to her? I don't even know her! I shrugged the kind feelings.

She could not hold back her tears this time and excused herself to the lavatory. I stood there waiting for her to return.

As we walked out of the Menagerie café, the sun casting long shadows on the cobblestones, I realized that this was not just an encounter over coffee. It was the start of something meaningful, a journey that had just begun.

And we both walked out quietly. There was something unsaid between us.

"I will see you at Burj Khalifa tomorrow at 9:30 a.m.," I said, keeping my distance and returning to my formal self as we entered the office.

Alia nodded and went in the opposite direction.

"So, how was your coffee?"

"It was great; Alia is indeed a beautiful person." He said and brightly smiled.

"So, do you like her?" I asked, poking a finger on Vinayak's shoulder and sitting on the desk near his chair.

"Maybe I do, but I'm indeed in love with her smile." He said, looking up at me.

I have a question: is it Love Jihad only when a Hindu girl falls in love with a Muslim guy, or is it also Love Jihad if a Hindu boy falls in love with a Muslim girl?" I asked in a sarcastic, teasing tone.

"Yes, it is Love Jihad and vice versa."

"Huh! So, did you ask her out?"

"No, she did." And he blushed smilingly.

"Did she?"

"She has to visit an orphanage near Burj Khalifa and I am bearing files for her."

The next day I arrived with a sense of anticipation. As I made my way to Burj Khalifa, the morning air was fresh and filled with the promise of a new beginning. The streets of Dubai were bustling, yet there was a certain tranquility in the way the city moved.

Arriving at the iconic skyscraper, I found Alia already waiting, her face illuminated by the early sunlight. She looked different today, perhaps more at ease, though there was still a hint of vulnerability in her eyes.

"Good morning," I greeted, trying to sound casual despite the fluttering in my chest.

"Morning," she replied with a soft smile, handing me a stack of files. "Ready to be my assistant for the day?"

I chuckled, "Absolutely. I've been practicing my file-holding skills all night."

We both laughed, and it felt as though a small barrier had been lifted between us. As we made our way towards the orphanage, the conversation flowed easily, touching upon everything from our favorite books to the quirks of living in a city as vibrant as Dubai.

At the orphanage, I watched Alia transform. Her warmth and sincerity shone through as she interacted with the children, her laughter mingling with theirs, filling the room with joy. It was a side of her I hadn't seen before, and it was captivating.

"You're amazing with them," I said as we took a break, sitting on a bench under the shade of a tree.

She shrugged modestly, "They just need someone to listen, to be there."

As the day wore on, I began to understand Alia a little more. Beneath the layers of professionalism and guardedness was a heart that cared deeply. The imprints she spoke of were still there, but they seemed to fade as she immersed herself in the present moment.

By the time we left, the sun was beginning to set, casting a golden hue over the city. We stood at the base of Burj Khalifa, the towering structure a silent witness to our day.

"Thank you for today," Alia said, her voice filled with gratitude and something else—perhaps hope.

"Thank you for letting me be a part of it," I replied, feeling a connection that was both unexpected and welcome.

As we parted ways, I realized that sometimes, the most meaningful journeys begin with the simplest of steps. And this was just the beginning. As the days passed, our newfound friendship blossomed, we both had different belief system and yet we were weaving life into the fabric of our daily lives. We found ourselves exploring the hidden gems of Dubai, from its lively souks to serene parks, each adventure strengthening the bond we were creating.

One afternoon, as we strolled along the Dubai Marina, the sun dipping below the horizon painted the sky in hues of pink and orange. Alia turned to me, her eyes reflecting the warmth of the setting sun. "You know," she began thoughtfully, "I never imagined finding someone who could see beyond the surface, who understands that there's always more to a person that meets the eye." "But why?"

I looked at her, questioningly.

"Why, do you believe people from different religion cannot have that deep connection, love or understanding to live a happy life?"

"I never said that!" But I also understood where she was going with the conversation.

"I believe when people are in love, they tend to do anything for their partner, they will not mind converting or transform their entire personality."

"So, you agree that if someone wants to change, they can change?" She emphasized on that change.

"Yes, but that transformation is short lived."

"How?"

Hmm, I sighed and took a deep breath.

"If Tanisha converts out of love after marriage, it will be a long, beautiful journey but if she choses to convert to marry Irtaka or converts after marrying Irtaka, she will start losing herself and the frustration will start building up. After a point, either she will give in to her frustration or that pain will kill her."

"But our religion is not that suffocating!" She said with pain in her eyes.

"I am not talking about religion, Alia. I am talking about how humans hate an imposing behavior."

"And it is not with her but every woman who marries, initially feels that suffocation. Why do you think marriages fall apart? Not all are Tanisha and Irtaka. It is because one partner is trying to be something that they are not and one partner is falling short in accepting the other." As I spoke my mind, I realized how rare and beautiful it was to connect with someone on such an authentic level.

With each passing day, Alia and I shared experiences and cherished each other's company. memories, and the city of Dubai, with its vibrant energy and endless possibilities, became the backdrop to a story of friendship, understanding, and growth.

And as we continued to have sweet coffee moments together, I realized that I was in love with Alia.

CHAPTER 20

"Bhai Jaan!" Alia stood at the room entrance. She was holding two coffee mugs in her hand. Irtaka looked at her over his favorite book of Ghalib Sahab and smiled.

"Come in, Alia," and he closed his book. Winds whistled as she crossed the window of the room.

Alia sat across Irtaka and looked at the book.

"Bhai Jaan, does love exist?" Fumbling with her dupatta. She waited for his reply.

"Existence depends on acknowledgment, and you cannot acknowledge something you do not believe in." Irtaka picked up his coffee mug and stood by the window, looking outside. "He is a good boy, Alia. Don't hold yourself back."

Alia looked at him, astonished and worried. "He is good, Bhai Jaan, but he does not know."

"Alia, you have come a long way. You are an educated, self-dependent, confident, and fantastic human being."

"Bhai Jaan, but when the truth is out?"

"Lifelong partnerships are based on love, care, sacrifices and, above all, acceptance."

"What if I am not accepted?"

"Alia, only a fool will not accept you. I am blessed to have you as my family; you will always be my family. Live your life and love without expectations. It won't hurt, and I am with you every step of the way. Don't look back, Alia; you are stronger than you think."

Alia hugged Irtaka and sobbed. Irtaka patted and kissed her head.

"You are Allah's special child. He tested you and will reward you with all His love. Believe in Him and let your heart love Him."

Alia wiped her tears and pulled back, giving Irtaka a heartfelt smile. "Thank you, Bhai Jaan," she whispered, feeling a renewed sense of courage and hope.

The room was filled with a comforting silence, the only sound being the gentle rustling of leaves outside. Alia took a sip of her coffee and felt the warmth spread through her, mirroring the warmth of her brother's words.

"Tomorrow," she said softly, "I'll talk to him. I need to be honest with myself and with him."

Irtaka nodded, his eyes filled with pride and encouragement. "That's the spirit, Alia. Whatever happens, remember that you are loved and cherished by those who truly matter."

With newfound determination, Alia felt ready to face whatever challenges lay ahead. She knew that, with her brother's unwavering support and the strength she found within herself, she could embrace the future with an open heart.

Alia stood at the majestic threshold of Burj Khalifa, the tallest marvel of human creation, as she beheld the joyous families streaming inside. A wave of warmth enveloped her, a testament to the profound bond of familial love.

Children, in their delightful exuberance, charmed her, yet their spirited antics can become a tad overwhelming. Adjusting his goggles, Vinayak requested the files, gesturing for her to take the lead.

"I wager you were a bit of a handful yourself in your youth," she teased, glancing at Vinayak.

"Good morning! Miss Alia."

"Good morning! Mr. Vinayak."

"So, are you equipped to manage those spirited youngsters?"

"Handling one at this very moment," she turned and beamed at him.

As they stepped onto the highest floor of Burj Khalifa, the view stopped Vinayak, and his jaw dropped. Alia held his hand and walked towards the glass window. "Every time I come here, I see new possibilities, new worlds, and untouched paths," Alia said, looking out of the open glass window.

Vinayak was quiet and observed Alia and the view with love. "You look happy!"

"Yes, this place makes me happy."

"And yet, something is holding you back."

"Mr. Vinayak, let me tell you a story today that my father narrated it to me when I was a kid."

"There was a man who had everything in his life. He had all the luxury and happiness, but he used to place a small pebble in his shoe."

"Why would he do that?"

"To remember God and feel gratitude towards Him in every step he took."

"So, you wish to keep the pebble with you intentionally?"

"Even if I wish to remove it, I cannot do it."

"Is it because you have started enjoying the pain or fear taking risks?"

Alia stood there numb, looking into his eyes. She wanted to say so much, but her mouth was sealed.

"Yes, this pain I am talking about. The pain in your eyes is ready to stream down, the pain that makes you vulnerable." He touched her hand and tilted his head, asking her to let go. "Don't hold back, Alia. The pain your heart cannot contain, and your soul won't forget, let it out and be mine. Let me touch your soul and love you. Be mine."

Alia just stood there.

"Please," he pleaded this time, "Let the wounds be left open."

"I am not so strong; Mr. Vinayak," Alia held him for support. She kept her hand on her chest, feeling the pain physically.

"Then let me be your strength." Vinayak held her arm, supporting and holding her.

"Excuse me, Miss. Are you alright?" A waiter asked Alia.

"Yes, she is good; she's just scared of heights," Vinayak said, looking at the waiter.

Alia moved quickly towards the exit lift, and Vinayak did not leave her. As the lift doors closed, Alia took a deep breath, trying to steady the storm of emotions swirling inside her. Vinayak stood silently by her side, his presence a comforting anchor in the midst of her turmoil.

The soft hum of the elevator was the only sound as it descended, and Alia felt a gentle warmth spreading from where Vinayak's hand rested on her arm. It was a warmth that whispered promises of healing, of understanding, and of a future unburdened by the pain of the past.

When the doors opened, they stepped out into the quiet lobby. The cool air was a welcome relief, and Alia paused, taking a moment to collect herself. Vinayak stayed close, his eyes filled with concern and unwavering support.

"Thank you," Alia murmured, her voice barely above a whisper. She looked at Vinayak, her eyes reflecting a mixture of gratitude and lingering fear. "I don't know what I would have done without you."

Vinayak smiled gently, his hand still holding hers. "You don't have to face this alone, Alia. I'm here, and I'm not going anywhere."

With those words, a small spark of hope ignited within her. For the first time in a long while, she felt the possibility of letting go, of embracing the present without being tethered to the past.

Together, they walked out into the evening, the cool breeze wrapping around them like a tender embrace. The world outside was alive with possibilities, and as they moved forward, Alia felt a sense of peace beginning to take root in her heart.

Alia broke into sobs sitting in the car and cried her heart out.

Vinayak sat there quietly watching her, handing over the tissues and waiting patiently for her to sober up.

"Alia, I love you!" He said, looking into her red eyes.

She said, between her sobs, "Why would you ever want to be with a girl like me?"

"A girl like you is a blessing; I would be a disaster without you." Alia looked at him, speechless.

"You don't know anything about me."

"I know enough to love you, Alia; you have a heart of gold."

"How can you be so sure about me?"

"Your voice has faith in Allah; your eyes see every man as equal."

Alia looked out of the window, her hands shaking. "Where would you like to go?"

"Home? Please take me home!" Alia said, teary eyes looking at Vinayak.

Alia sat on the couch and stared blankly at the family picture.

"Water," Vinayak offered the glass and sat beside her. "Thank you!" She said after a long pause.

"I like your family pictures; I wanted one for myself, but I am from a very low-income family in Malaysia."

"I was 13 years old, playing with my younger brother on our farmland. One day, my parents came with two men, heavily built and well-dressed. My parents were thrilled and offered them the best food we had in our house."

"My father came close to me and said, 'These people will take you to a school. It is an all-girls' school, and you will be educated in Dubai.' I was excited and joyous because I had always dreamt of having books and being in a school. My mother's happiness was beyond measure as she packed my bag."

"As we were about to leave, I was holding on to my mother's gown and did not want to leave her. I had tears in my eyes and could not see anything. The next moment, I heard a loud sound and turned around to see my father lying on the ground, lifeless. My mother ran towards him, and I followed her, but the next bullet shot went through her head, and she fell to the ground. I was running towards her when the men grabbed me and muffled my mouth. I saw the other men taking a shot towards my younger brother, and before I could do or say anything, I heard the third gunshot. That was the first time in my life I felt death. I saw my parents and little brother lying dead in the stream of blood. The next thing I remember was that I was thrown in the trunk of the car, and darkness is all I recall."

"I did not see sunlight for a few days and always felt weak, lost, and dizzy. I had no energy.

Then, one day, I saw a girl close to me. We were in a closed, dark room, but before I could comprehend anything, I was grabbed and stripped naked and thrown into the rustic old bathroom, and a jet sprayed cold water on my bare skin. That day, shivering in that dark place, I saw and felt fear: dark, wet, and cold. Slowly, I understood I was not in any educational center. I was sold to the highest bidder, who was an older man. A 13-year-old girl was scared.

Little did I know that was the beginning of the worst days. I was sold to an animal in human form. He was a sadist; he did things to me unimaginable to the human mind. He burned my skin and would peel it off slowly. The more I portrayed pain, the more he felt aroused.

I survived the brutality to witness the worst the next day. I wanted to die. The irony of life is that I stayed because every time I was being tortured or was played around by men. I imagined myself free and happy in my pastured lands, and that hope kept me alive. I was caged for years; I had no idea of the day or the time. I had not spoken in a long while."

"One day, I was put on a table offering food while the men would toss the food on my body and eat it, biting me. The fork stabs were painful. It would pierce my flesh and make me cringe, but the more pain I would display, the more forks were stabbed. One day, the pain was excruciating, and I was," she paused momentarily. "I picked the fork from the table and pierced it into the neck of a person. I don't remember who and before someone could hold me. I did the same for the other two men with him, covered myself with whatever I could find, and ran for my life. I remember running senselessly through the corridors down the stairs and hearing the footsteps following me. I was scared and ran thoughtlessly. I saw a man opening his car, and I extended the back door and hid myself in the back seat. The man turned and was shocked at what he witnessed, but seeing other men in the parking, he understood and raced the car to without a question."

"After driving for a long time, he stopped the car in the desert."

"He offered me some water and clothes. He went back to his driving seat and drove without asking any questions. Days later, I opened my eyes and saw myself in a soft bed, cleaned and being medicated. The man who had rescued me was sitting beside me. I noticed pain in his eyes and sympathy for me. For the first time in my life, someone had ever looked at me as a human. That day, I cried for the years of pain I had endured.

Irtaka Bhai Jaan rescued me and nursed me back to health. He would stay close to me, pray all day by my bedside, wait for me to wake up, and sit there with me, looking out the window at the clear sky."

Vinayak sat there without moving, and Alia stared blankly and said nothing.

Vinayak stood up, walked to the window, and said, "Whatever I said earlier made me realize my mistake."

Alia looked at him sacred! "I understand if a man does not want to be with me!"

"No," Vinayak knelt before her in speeding light and held her hand. "After listening to what you just said, I have realized how wrong I was about you being soft and fragile, where as you are a warrior who has endured pain to an extreme and still hold the kindness in every word you speak. You did not let them touch your soul. And I love you. It is not just a feeling, but all my thoughts are to be part of your life and be by your side forever."

"Vinayak, it won't be easy!" Alia exclaimed. "Alia! It will be our journey of love."

"I should leave! It's getting darker and more complex."

He held her hand and looked emotionally, waiting for her reply. Alia took a deep breath, her eyes reflecting the myriads of emotions swirling within her. She knew the path ahead was fraught with challenges, yet she felt a warmth and sense of safety in Vinayak's presence that she had never known before.

With a gentle squeeze of his hand, she whispered, "Vinayak, I am scared of what the future holds, but I believe in us. Together, we can face anything. Your love has given me strength, and I am ready to embark on this journey with you."

Vinayak's heart soared with her words. He pulled her into a tender embrace, feeling grateful for the chance to be with someone as extraordinary as Alia. In that moment, they both understood that love, with all its trials and triumphs, was worth pursuing.

As they stood by the window, the looking at the moonlight they silently promised to support each other, their journey had just begun, and with each other's love as their guiding light, they were ready to face whatever the future might hold.

When Tanisha and Irtaka came home, they were happy to see them. Upon seeing Irtaka, "Bhai Jaan," she pulled her hand from Vinayak's hand.

"Alia, you are a free bird, and Vinayak is a good person." He placed his hand on her head approving their union.

"I will still take time to approve you, Mr. Irtaka," he smiled, walked closer, and hugged him after a momentary pause. "I wish I could say you are as lucky as I am; Tanisha is a complex, crazy woman to be with. You have my sympathies."

He saw a pillow coming his way and, ducked and ran around the hall playfully.

Alia and Irtaka sat on the sofa, witnessing our catfight before we sat for dinner. The dinner table had a variety of food and emotions. Laughter echoed through the room as everyone took their seats, the tension from earlier slowly dissipating into the warmth of shared companionship. The aroma of spices and freshly cooked dishes filled the air, promising a delightful feast.

As we settled in, Tanisha began serving the dishes, her eyes sparkling with happiness. "I hope you all brought your appetites," she chimed, passing a bowl of fragrant biryani to Alia, who smiled appreciatively.

Irtaka raised his glass, his voice steady and filled with gratitude. "To new beginnings and cherished friendships," he toasted, his gaze sweeping across the table to rest on Alia and Vinayak. "May we always find strength in unity and love in every moment we share."

I felt a renewed sense of hope, clinked my glass with Alia's, whispering, "Here's to our journey, wherever it may lead us."

Alia nodded, her eyes swelling up with a mixture of emotions. Though the path ahead was uncertain but she felt confident and sense of belonging amongst us, new friends who had swiftly become family.

CHAPTER -21

We all gathered around the dinner table, suspended in uncertainty about the future, crafting our own little universe while seeking joy.

My gaze fell upon Alia and Vinayak, who were placing their trust in fate. I could sense the effort Alia was making to appear joyful and self-assured. The shadows of her past lingered, yet when I turned to Vinayak, I recognized a genuinely good soul.

Only humanity can dictate one's character. How long will different belief systems wreak havoc upon us? How long will it be wielded as a tool for division, fueling hatred and envy—a legacy of nations torn apart by conflict and bloodshed, fracturing humanity? Even religion is often employed to satiate our egos and craft superior identities in society under the guise of divine will.

Tanisha, a Hindu, finds herself pursued by her own kin. Alia, a Muslim, has suffered at the hands of hers.

It is the mighty who suppress the meek. The only true religion that endures is humanity itself, with faith merely a way of life.

As I surveyed my surroundings, I whispered gratitude to Allah for the blessings cascading upon us, shielding us from the harshness of the world and bestowing us with strength for fresh beginnings.

Yet, concern for Tanisha's safety gnawed at me, but that was not the entirety of my worry.

Alia and I sat in the car, her fingers dancing nervously in silence. Letting go of her fears proved a challenge as she gazed out the window.

"Bhai Jaan, Abu?" She asked, encapsulating a multitude of worries in a single word. "Yes, Abu will embrace him!"

"Bhai Jaan, does he know about Tanisha Baji?"

I was still pondering! As I sped along the road, thoughts swirled about how to broach the subject with Abu. He had been my friend, my guide, my unwavering supporter, and my honest critic. He wished for Imtiyaz and me to embody goodness, but accepting our differences was a different journey. I would share that I had fallen for someone from another faith, a vibrant culture, a distinct language, divergent thoughts, and a lifestyle separate from our own. I was enchanted by this difference.

Early the next morning, I approached Abu's room, the floral fragrance transporting me back to moments when Dad would sit at the table, imparting Arabic lessons to Imtiyaz and me.

"Irtaka," he called, "Child, come here!"

"Salam Abu, how is your health? How are you feeling today?"

"Iinaa bikhayr ,iinaa jayid. How are you Irtaka? Come sit near me."

I sat near his bedside and kissed his hands. I looked at the gold ring just above the scar that was healing.

I said nothing and sat there, watching him grow old and weak.

"Abu, I need to tell you something."

"Come closer, dear, and say your heart."

"Abu, I have not been fair with Tabeeya. She has dedicated her life to this house. She looks at me for acceptance."

Abu looked at me and smiled, keeping his hand on my shoulder.

"Yes, you have been hard on Tabeeya, Irtaka. But you were looking out for your brother.

"Tabeeya respects you and looks up to you."

Abu looked at me and smiled again, this time with a question.

"What made you realize that you need to apologize to Tabeeya?" He asked.

"Abu," I paused, looking him in the eye, and thought, what if he disapproves of Tanisha?

"Abu! I realized it but could not find the courage." I tried changing the topic.

"Abu Jaan! He is in love!" Imtiyaz entered and hugged me. "Only a person in love can understand dedication and sacrifice for the family."

Abu looked at me with wide eyes, smiled wide, and opened his arms to hug me. I took his hands, kissed them, and hugged him.

"Is that true, Irtaka? Are you in love?"

"Yes! Abu."

"Who is the girl?"

I lost my heartbeat for a second. I had never been so scared to tell him.

"Who is she?" He asked with love.

I had no words and knew this was the time to man up. "Abu, her name is Tanisha, 'Tanisha Oberoi'."

"Tanisha, Masha Allah!" He came forward and kissed my forehead. "Abu, she is Hindu and Indian!"

Abu had a concerned face. He saw me with a smile and stood up to pour his tea. He was stirring his tea, but clearly, he was somewhere else. "Sometimes history should not be repeated," he said, looking at us hurtfully. After a long pause, he stated, "We have to make amends to it," handing me the tea.

He poured another cup for Imtiyaz and sat in his chair.

Imtiyaz and I looked at him and wondered what he meant. Our curiosity grew with every second, but we sipped our tea silently.

"Do you remember your grandparents?" He smiled at us.

"Yes, Grandpa and Grandma loved us visiting them in Pakistan." Imtiyaz shifted in his chair and sipped his tea.

"They were not my birth parents."

Imtiyaz and I looked at each other, a bit confused.

"I lost my parents at birth. Father died in Indo-War, and mother in childbirth. I was raised by my parents, Mohammad Raza Sahab and Bibi Rida."

Imtiyaz looked at me, a bit concerned.

"And then, I went to Yale University for my higher studies. My vali and ami had always shown me a more excellent vision that needed to be worked on. I excelled in every area of my life but felt incomplete until I met your mother. She was different from me in every manner. She was American with a sense of cultural importance, and that combination was very diverse. It was her curiosity towards religion, how religion makes life easier, how families abide by religion and how the rules of every family member are sorted. She argued on points that made me think we would have endless discussions on how life could be perfected and how every family member had an essential role in running a family. It was as if we met each other and had fallen in love.

We got married right after college. I got a job at Dubai University, so I decided to settle in Dubai from Pakistan, and she followed me just the way men and women are told to do. But moving to Dubai was a step back for both of us, an orthodox country where her life changed drastically; but she never complained. She wanted to be with me by my side no matter where life would take us.

But things changed for us. I was the head of the ethics department, where theory and practice were different. It was much easier to have a taste for modernization among the modern people, but amid the orthodox people, where their wife's uncovered head was a big issue. It was difficult for your mother, but she did everything for me. Your mother was of liberal thought when she dressed, but for us, she started making amends and did everything to keep us together. I could not see what was happening. I was different; my words and actions differed. I thought I had balanced my life but was blind to the slow poison creeping into our lives. She was dying inside. The poison was killing her willpower, her self-confidence, her smile, and her happiness, and the poison made me blind; I could not see it. I was blind to her pain and struggle. I was blind to us; I was blind to everything, and even when she was pregnant and when she needed me the most, I was not there."

He had tears in his eyes. I knew Dad blamed himself for our mother's death, but why did he never tell us? We knew Mom was from the state they had met in the university, fell in love, married, and shifted to Dubai.

He continued, "It was after we married and shifted to Dubai that I changed. I could not stand up for her, her lifestyle, or her wishes. All she asked for was my time and my love. I was proving my masculinity in society by being the head, abiding by the rules, and inviting her to change as per society. She sacrificed everything, thinking I would love her after she had done as per my wishes, but I demanded more, and she sacrificed more. She did everything I wanted but nothing that she liked. It killed her from the inside. I was never there for her when she was expecting you both. I did not praise her; I did not love her, and it killed her.

After she gave birth, she was weak. The doctor said she could be revived if she had the willpower, but that's what I had destroyed: her willpower. She could not anticipate me changing or her future. She was tired of waiting and being hurt by the one who had promised to love and care for her and stand by her side. I had broken her trust and her heart, and it was only me who made her think that death was much easier than life."

This confession was the deepest cut to his soul. He loved her, but being the reason for her death, he loathed himself. He stumbled, and Imtiaz held him. We made him sit on the chair, and he gasped for air. He sobbed in Imtiyaz's arms.

"When your mother died, history repeated itself. I felt every inch of pain that you would endure as children, and I did everything for you. I decided to raise you without a mother and care for you two like my parents did."

Abu looked at me and said, "Losing your mother was the same pain I had gone through, but I will not let you repeat the history of losing your love."

"Today, you are in love! In the same manner, I was in love with your mother because she was different. She had a voice to her thoughts. She was a risk taker yet cared immensely. She had a charm because she was pure at heart. They never let religion be a barrier, but as strength, she was God-loving, not God-fearing. She used to love and would do anything for her loved ones. But I ruined the most precious relationship I had."

He spoke after a long pause.

"She was a beautiful soul. Even on her deathbed bed, she requested me to be present for you both and love you both unconditionally. She asked me never to let anything like this happen to the girls who would marry our boys."

When Tabeeya came, I saw how Imtiyaz was by her side and was proud. "And now it's your turn, Irtaka." He looked at me with those pearly eyes.

"Promise me, Irtaka, that you will never ask her to change; you will not repeat my mistakes."

I hugged him because I had no words; I felt relieved, light, and happy. I wanted to bring Tanisha home now more than ever. Imtiyaz hugged us and crunched both of us in his arms.

"We have waited so long for this moment." Tabeeya and Alia entered with the room.

Everything was so perfect today, and I looked at Alia and she smiled and hid behind Tabeeya.

Abu looked at us and wondered?

"Abu, I think I have found a good boy for Alia!"

Abu! smiled and looked at her, raising his hands. "Alhamdulillah! Alhamdulillah! Alhamdulillah!"

Imtiyaz looked at me, all confused but happy, and kissed Alia on her forehead. Tabeeya stood there quietly, a bit uncertain but happy.

"Who is he?" Abu asked.

"Abu, it's Tanisha's brother Vinayak," I said, looking at him. Abu sat in the chair, lost for a few seconds.

"Abu," I went near him and looked at him questioningly. "What is wrong?"

Abu looked at me and asked if he was a good person. I held his hand and assured him.

"Does he know everything?"

I nodded my head and called Alia near me.

Alia sat near Abu, and he cupped her face in his hands. "Dear, do you like him?" He asked.

Alia nodded, and with teary eyes, she buried her face in his hands. "Alhamdulillah! Alhamdulillah! Alhamdulillah!"

"You are a blessed child of Allah; live your life, dear."

Abu had teary eyes; the pain of a father on the thought of marrying his daughter is a mixed feeling.

Imtiyaz approached Abu and put his hands on his shoulder, feeling emotional. Tabeeya stood at a distance and cried happy tears.

"So, Bhai Jaan, when are we meeting Tanisha and his brother?" Abu looked at me for the same answer.

"Soon, but before that, I wish to apologize for my behavior! Please forgive me, Tabeeya. I want to be the best person for the baby."

CHAPTER 22

As the final day of inaugural for the foundation project came, we all gathered on the cruise to celebrate and share the newfound love among us.

I was meeting his father for the first time today and I hope he likes me. The excitement was making me anxious as the cruise was anchored over the gentle waves, the sun setting in a blaze of colors that mirrored the emotions in my heart. I stood nervously at the edge of the deck, the cool breeze ruffling my hair, as I awaited the moment I would meet his father.

I had heard so much about his father—a man of wisdom and kindness, whose approval meant the world to Irtaka. I wanted nothing more than to make a good impression, but I knew nothing of their culture.

Laughter and music filled the air as guests were boarding the ship. The atmosphere was joyous, a fitting backdrop for both the professional and personal milestones we were celebrating.

As I took a deep breath, preparing myself to meet the man, I realized that this was more than just an introduction—it was a new chapter, a blending of our lives and families. Irtaka's father approached, his eyes warm and inviting, and in that moment, I knew everything would be alright.

"Mr. Khan," I greeted him with a respectful nod, "it's an honor to finally meet you."

He smiled, and I could see the pride in his eyes. "The honor is mine, Tanisha. Welcome to the family," and he hugged me with all his fatherly love.

With those words, any lingering nerves dissipated, replaced by a sense of belonging and love. The journey ahead felt bright and promising.

Abu kept moving forward with his assistant and observed all the decorations very minutely. I kept hoping he liked every bit of it, and suddenly, I was pulled back by Alia.

"Miss Tanisha, you look gorgeous, and I completely understand why my brother fell in love with you!" She had accompanied Abu.

"Likewise," and we blushed, suppressing our smiles.

"The boat is an excellent choice for the party; it gives us more time with office renovations. How many guests have arrived? I asked her.

"Almost everyone!"

Irtaka entered with a pregnant woman. I recalled seeing her somewhere.

"Alia, who is she?"

"Oh! She is Tabeeya Baaji."

I looked at Alia and what she had just said. "Baaji?"

"You know her?" I asked her, dying inside.

"Yeah, she is his wife."

I looked at Alia astonished! "Any problem, Miss Tanisha."

I looked at her with my whole life hanging by the thread. "What is her name again?"

"Tabeeya."

Irtaka and Tabeeya—"IT", I was shaken and held Alia for support. I looked at Alia again and was shocked by her calm face.

"Do you know about her?"

"Yes, I thought you knew her too!"

She looked a bit shocked by my reaction.

How could I forget that their religion allows them to marry twice, but that's not the point? I was unaware of it, and "IT" stands for Irtaka and Tabeeya. There must be a misunderstanding or a mistake; I was trying to explain it to myself. What mistake can there be? He was entering and holding his wife—his pregnant wife. My inner self kept shouting at me.

"Would you like something to drink?" Alia looked at me, a bit concerned.

I ignored her, my eyes red with tears. I walked to the bar section, tears rolling down my cheeks, and grabbed the glass of scotch the waiter was filling for the guests. I gulped it neatly in one go, but the betrayal had more heat than the neat scotch.

I picked another, and the screeching path it took in my throat made me cry louder. I chose another because I just wanted to time out from the film repeating in a loop in my head.

The film of betrayal and being fooled.

I took another, and by this time, the waiter slipped the glasses away and offered me water. I stomped my way out from the exit level of the ship, which had a parking lot near it.

I walked, crying, and felt the betrayal knife stabbed in my back, and it was ridiculously hurting in physical form. I sat in the middle of nowhere, screaming, yelling, and looking around. I tried standing up and felt everything blur.. There was a bright light, and I fell again.

I don't want to get up; I am broken. He cheated on me. He has a wife, and she is pregnant. My God, my Lord, will never forgive me for what injustices I have done to that unborn child; God, how could I ever face her or the child?

Is this Jihad? My mind portrayed the ugly picture, intensifying my fears, and I cried uncontrollably. This is not love; I just wanted to die at that moment. I could not think of what I would say to Vinayak, Didi, or myself. I won't be able to face myself in the mirror. Vinayak was right, and I was dumb enough to fight him.

"Tanisha!"

"Open your eyes! Are you all right?"

"Is she drunk?"

"Didi!"

I am dead, I am hearing them cry over my body.

"No, you're not dead idiot, you are drunk," Kashvi slapped me.

"No, I want to die. I cannot handle this betrayal."

"Irtaka, pick her up, and let's go."

"No, he will not touch me. He is a married man."

"What?" Didi and Irtaka both shouted together.

"Yes, he is married, di. He lied to me. I saw him and his wife, and she was pregnant."

"And you are crazy, Tanisha."

"Di, I saw them together. It's all a lie. Why did he not tell me about his wife?"

"Irtaka, she is not in her sense; let's go."

"Yes, I was not in my sense because I loved this man; I drooled over his one glance. All I wanted was him; I opened my heart to him. I could fight the world for him, but he betrayed me.

He said he loved me. I believed him because I wanted it to be true. Ah! My head Di, I can't take this pain— it's hurting badly, Di, badly. I will die, I'll die. Just take me home, please. I won't come back here ever. I don't want to be here even for a second; please take me home."

She hugged me, and I cried in her arms and passed out.

Back in the room, I was coming back to my senses but unwilling to. I should have taken more shots of the sinful drink; I was crying. I don't know if it was real or my dreams.

"Shhh! I am here, and I'll not leave your side." Irtaka held me closer in his arms, and I struggled to open my eyes.

"Why did you lie to me?" I started to sob in an exhausted state, "And now, I feel guilty in the eyes of your first wife and her unborn child. I was supposed to know Irtaka."

"Tanisha, I swear I have not lied to you about anything."

"I saw you with her; you cannot lie to me, Irtaka. Don't lie to me."

"I won't, and I can't even imagine lying to you, Tanisha. You are my love and my life."

"But you lied and are lying to me again, Irtaka. And "IT" means Irtaka and Tabeeya."

"Tanisha, I feel accused of a crime I have not committed."

"Yet! Because we did not get married; it would be a sin if I got married to you."

"Tanisha STOP! Just stop now. I have loved you ever since I saw you!"

"You saw me few months ago, but IT has been way before me."

"I have loved you since I saw you, and that was not the day I noticed you on the flight."

"What? What does that mean?"

He went quieter than ever and looked grave. What did he mean by that? What's wrong with him?

"Nothing! Yeah, nothing, because you have no excuse. How can I ever understand you, especially since you show me your love, your concern, and at times, I have no idea what you are talking about."

He held me closer to him, and it was a different way that I had seen him. He was scared, and there was something he still wanted to hide.

"You have to speak; you can't keep quiet and hide things."

"I love you," he held me in his embrace.

"Irtaka, what are you hiding from me? If you say she is not your wife, who is she, and what were you doing with her? What's the big thing that you are hiding? Why are you hiding 'IT' from me?"

"You don't know me at all! Tanisha," he held me in his arms, gripped me tightly, and looked deep into my eyes; his eyes had so much to say. His lips moved to express something, but he could not speak.

"Please, Irtaka, say it; I want to know what you're holding back." I wept, tears streaming down my face, and I dug my head into his chest. I always feel safe in his arms, even though he is married. "Please, Irtaka, tell me, I want to know everything."

He pulled back and looked at me with tears in his eyes.

"I knew your mother." he looked into my eyes and stood stiff.

"Wha.. What! You knew my mother! My mother is dead and was in India and never came to Dubai. Don't cover Irtaka. Please don't use my parents to save us. Tell me the truth."

"Yes, I knew her."

It was all a shock to me, and I was just speechless. I tried to sit, but I could not move. I had frozen; I was scared. I was attempting to comprehend the words and what I had heard. I looked up at Irtaka as if he was pointing to something suspicious.

I looked at him. He moved and made me sit on the bed. He posed in front of me because he was not finished.

"Irtaka, you knew everything this entire time and chose not to tell me."

"You were not copping up with their death, and telling you the truth was not what we wanted. That's when we decided to move you to another country."

"We? Who are we?"

"Your sister and I, Kaashvi, suggested I offer you a job in my company."

"Kaashvi asked you to provide me a job."

"Yes, I did because you had stopped living your life, and we all chose to hide from you because Mom said it," Kaashvi added.

"Mom said it?" I looked at her angrily.

"Irtaka was her student, and she even knew his feelings for you."

I looked at Di! With tears in my eyes, I did not move because I was stunned. I felt like my own family had snubbed me.

"Mom told me not to say anything to you. She informed me that you are fragile and look at the world with love, and Irtaka did what he could in the best manner to heal you and protect you from unknown harms."

"And Mom and Dad did were killed, and they knew what was coming, for they were soldiers."

"What!" I was shocked by her words. "You are saying that they knew! What was coming, and they did not die but were killed?"

"Yes, Tanisha, they were killed."

Tears turned into sobs, and I could not hold it anymore.

"So, it was not love. It was all charity from him, my own family hiding things from me because they think I am weak and I need to be protected by concealing the truth."

Di hugged me, wiped my tears and made me sit.

"No Tanisha, not at all, you are loved by all of us. Mom had stumbled on the idea of Love Jihad being used by the extremists who had decided to start Hindu-Muslim riots to win the upcoming elections.

Thousands would have died if they had not exposed the leaders, and that's what had made them the target."

"Exposed?"

"Yes. They knew who those people were, and those people knew Mom and Dad were going to expose them; that's what killed them."

"The incident created turmoil, and the people backed off from their intentions. They did not die for nothing. Like a true soldier, Dad saved many lives, and Mom kept her promise to live and die with Dad and be a soldier's wife."

"She had anticipated all these from the research data that Irtaka had collected. Many people talked to Irtaka, thinking that he is Muslim and from Dubai, who would not only agree to them but also fund them.

Irtaka did not understand the intentions, but Mom understood all the conspiracy and informed Dad.

As the day they passed, they came home and told me everything and the consequences that could arise.

And that evening, we got the news.

Then, Irtaka showed up after a few months. Mom had told me about him, and I suggested he help me send you away for a change. Also, I was worried about you learning the truth."

By now, Irtaka was sitting on the bed by my side and holding me.

He has been following the attacks on you and they all narrowed to hate groups wanting to harm Irtaka personally.

Vinayak, did he know? I asked.

"After the accident, he was suspicious, and after you left, all he did was dig for clues. To stop him, I gave him a half-cooked truth, but he was relentless. I begged him to stop, but he would not listen, and that's when he learnt that you have feelings for Irtaka. He was scared for you, and so he came to Dubai. He wanted to protect you."

"And then, seeing him unstable, Irtaka talked to him on the road trip."

"Where is he now? And when did you guys fly here?" I asked, a little present in the moment.

"It was supposed to be a surprise for you at the party, but it is no longer a surprise." And she hugged me and kissed me. I sat in her arms, sobbing and missing Mom and Dad dearly even more.

Kaashvi, left the room after I sobered up, and Irtaka sat beside me.

"I am sorry!"

"I wish I could change all of that."

I hugged him because I knew Mom had approved him; if she had, Dad had to. I was happy to learn my parents had approved my choice. "I love you".

He said nothing but tightened his hug, indicating he loved me more. "There is something I wish to show and tell you."

"I hid part of my love because I didn't know how to tell you," and he said with a heavy sigh. "I was 13 years old when Dad started taking us to India to pay our homage to Ajmer sheriff. I grew older, and I missed my mother. As people say, small kids stay attached to their mothers at a tender age, and I was no different, but the year I turned 14, I started to show symptoms of Depression. My father took me to Ajmer Sharif, asking for my well-being before he began my therapy. That was the year I begged God to please give me a reason to stay in this world. I had heard people say that if God takes away someone's mother, then Allah provides them with an angel that will love them, protect them, and be on their side always. I begged Allah to give me my angel."

"It was the morning prayer time. I prayed, and we sat there in the area. I had closed my eyes and was busy begging to send me my angel, and I wished to see my angel. I prayed and implored Allah after Namaz for the whole time. It was silent everywhere.

Tanisha! This sound made me open my eyes. It was as if the Lord asked me to open my eyes and see my angel; there you stood in front of me, a white face with red cheeks, eyes green and brown hair, your perfect smile would heal any heart. The aura around you glowed and was more potent than the faith.

You were 11, but I knew you were my angel. Then I learnt your mother and my father had studied together in Yale; she was her batch mate and understood my mother well. When she knew of my depression and, she offered her help. We would talk lengths online, and she would love me like her child.

I went to Dargah Ajmer Shareef every year to see that angelic spirit. Every year, I met your mother and father; for hours, she would narrate stories about you. Then, three years ago, we planned to have a joint research project.

At that time, I was madly in love with you but could not risk losing you, so I kept quiet.

Your mother realized my love for you but she said she would let you choose what you want in life.

I did everything possible to ensure you listened to your heart and chose your desires. It was your mother's wish that you follow your heart and decide what you like. I did not know what you felt, and honoring your mother's wish and my promise to her was essential for me.."

I looked into his eyes and fell in love all over him again.

"IT has always meant Irtaka and Tanisha." He kissed my forehead. "I could not say anything until I knew what you felt for me."

I looked blankly at him and then realized that there was still something he was going to say. "And?"

"I love you," and he held me tighter in his embrace.

Picking up the shattered energy, I asked again, "And?"

"And that lady you saw is not my wife; she is my sister-in-law Tabeeya, my brother's wife and it was my brother, Imityaz with her, not me."

"Your brother looked so similar."

"Yes, we are twins."

"What? When were you going to tell me that?"

"Irtaka," I whispered his name and embraced him. "I am so sorry."

"Tabeeya met you in the store but asked me not to tell you anything; she wanted to meet you only when things were official with me."

He pulled a picture from his pocket and showed it to me. I recognized Tabeeya, his dad, but could not tell the difference between him and his brother.

"You both look so similar; shit, I was so stupid."

"May I request one thing?" He looked into my eyes warmly, "Promise that you will not think of yourself as a victim of Jihadi Love because that shatters me; I don't want you to change for me. I want you to be free and live your life with me. I want us to be one soul."

I hugged him with all my strength and nodded with sobs.

"What if I had fallen in love with someone else?" I asked between my sobs.

"I would have just made sure you got the one you love!"

"But it's good I fell in love with you," and I tried smiling with my half sobs, teary red eyes, and running nose.

"And your love has raised me to my best," and we snuggled into each other's arms.

As I stood at the deck making peace with Mom and Dad being gone, I looked at the deep sea.

"How are you," Vinayak asked as he joined me at the deck.

I turned to face him, offering a small, grateful smile.

"I'm better now," I replied softly, feeling the gentle sway of the ship beneath us. "It's been a whirlwind of emotions, but I'm starting to find my footing again."

Vinayak nodded, his expression a mix of understanding and concern.

"I was worried about you, you know. But seeing you here, standing strong, gives me hope."

I leaned against the railing, the salt-tinged breeze brushing against my skin. "It hasn't been easy," I admitted, "but I have so much support around me. And the truth, as painful as it was, has also brought a sense of clarity and relief."

Vinayak joined me in gazing out at the endless horizon, the sun dipping lower, painting the sky in hues of orange and pink. "Mom and Dad would be proud," he said softly. "Proud of how you're handling everything, how you're finding strength even in your weakest moments."

A warmth spread through my chest at his words, a reassurance that I was on the right path. "Thank you, Vinayak. It means a lot to hear you say that."

We stood in comfortable silence, the sounds of the celebration drifting in the background. The sea was vast and mysterious, much like the journey ahead, but I felt ready to embrace whatever came my way. With Vinayak and the others by my side, and with love guiding my heart, I knew I would be okay.

"Can I ask you something?"

"Yes," he looked at me.

"You really love Alia?"

"Yes, why do you ask?"

"Then what changed your mind and made you love a person from another religion?"

"Someone has to keep the count," he said without emotions and left.

I stood there, numb, at his words echoing in my head.

ABOUT THE AUTHOR

Tripti Dutta is a vibrant soul who artfully intertwines creativity with entrepreneurship. A burgeoning author and astute businesswoman, she also uncovers her artistic flair as a DJ. Tripti aspires to wield her literary voice as a catalyst for transformation.

In her debut novel, she boldly confronts the deeply rooted patriarchal mindsets, challenging societal norms and championing the vision of a more equitable world. This imaginative tale draws from the haunting injustices and biases she has witnessed in her surroundings.

Her writing invites readers to contemplate societal imperfections and forge a path toward a more just and empathetic community, establishing her as not just a storyteller, but a true agent of change.

www.ingramcontent.com/pod-product-compliance
Lightning Source LLC
LaVergne TN
LVHW041909070526
838199LV00051BA/2560